From *Flares* *Amidst Shadows* Productions

過去からの影
ASOYA

Shadows From the Past

過去からの影

Asoya

Shadows From the Past

（過去からの影）

Joseph DaVaulia

XULON PRESS

Xulon Press
2301 Lucien Way #415
Maitland, FL 32751
407.339.4217
www.xulonpress.com

Unless otherwise indicated, Scripture quotations taken from the King James Version (KJV)–*public domain*.

Printed in the United States of America.

ISBN-13: 978-1-6305-0554-7

Contents

Section 1

The Blade, the Past and the Word...................... 1

Ninja and Shadows 3

The Season of Netsu, Summer 5

Mr. Yutaka and the Bookie 11

Elisa.. 19

Asoya's Trip to the Orphanage 24

Asoya Rejected By the Town's People 27

Sin and Shadows..................................... 31

The Nine Paid Assailants 35

Asoya Drops a Large Bag of Food Off at the Orphanage..... 44

Asoya and the Word Carrier Before Him 48

Asoya's Followed 51

Ruthless Vermillion.................................. 54

Elisa's Counsel 61

The Shadow 64

Section 2

The Condemnation, the Revelation, and the Salvation 73

The Old Nature 75

Solitude 77

Asoya's Trip 79

The Following Morning 85

The Medicine Man and The Light 90

The Apple and Sugegasa 94

Heart Check 100

Asoya and the Fisherman 109

Asoya's Past 115

Remember 119

The Truth and the Shield 127

Asoya Victorious! 137

The Golden Plated Throwing Star 139

Word Carriers and Candles 146

About the Writer/Illustrator 153

過去からの影
Section 1

The Blade, the Past and the Word

過去　　　ブレード　　　言葉

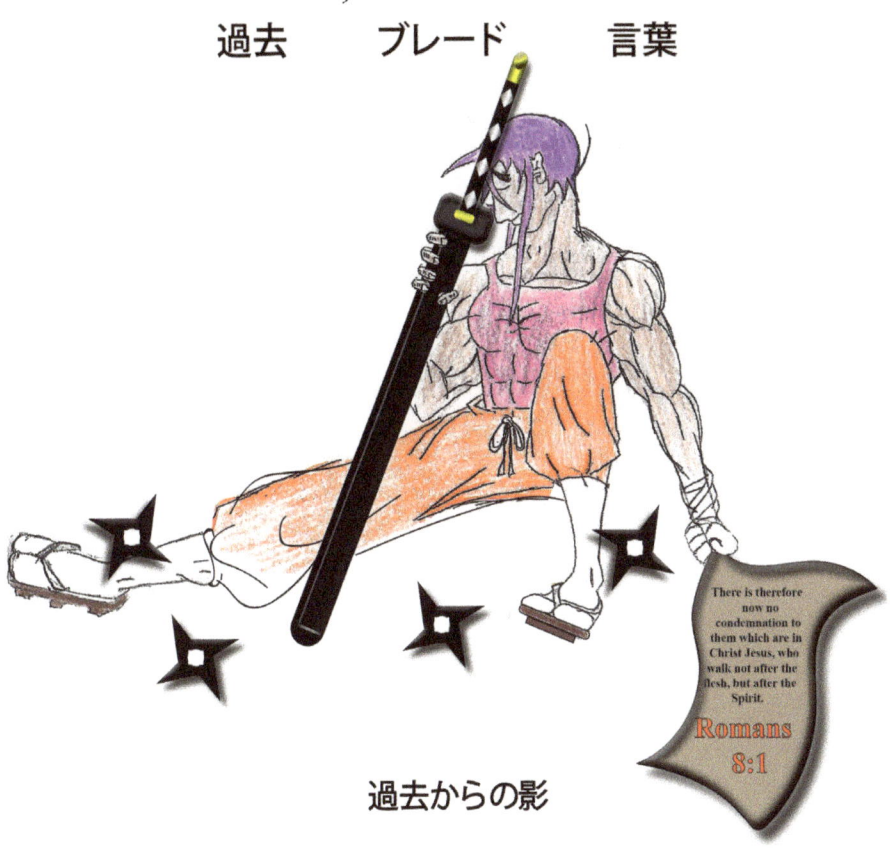

There is therefore now no condemnation to them which are in Christ Jesus, who walk not after the flesh, but after the Spirit.

Romans 8:1

過去からの影

Ninja and Shadows 影

Everything has a core, something that make it what it is and function the way that it does. For ninja it is a specific set of teachings that guides them, a philosophy 哲学. The core philosophy of those who are titled ninja is to do everything that has been ordered until it is complete, and those orders must be done in the shadows. Many things are done in the night, amidst the darkness, where the light of the sun has fled and the shine that comes from the moon and the innumerable stars is pushed back just enough for the shadows to appear.

Ninjas use the shadows as part of their craft. It cloaks them. They have no autonomy, no personal freedoms or liberties apart from their clan. They are forged into weapons, and as weapons they slay. Shadows are more than just the night or shade. They are things that are hidden…intentions. Concerning ninjas, nothing assuages them, these agents of confidentiality…shadows…assassins.

There is a ninja who left the shadows to walk in the light. His name is Asoya. Since leaving the clan, Asoya has learned *autarky*

3

自給 自足: the art of being independent or self-sufficient, apart from the clan…independent from the will of that clan's master. This terrain has been foreign to him, but like all techniques that are learned, Asoya is adjusting.

The Season of Netsu, Summer

“It is summer yet again,” Asoya says calmly, walking past a tree filled with the cherries known as *sakuranbo*. He reaches his hand up and picks a few, just enough to fit in his hand. The *sakuranbo* tree's leaves are just the shade he needs to shield him momentarily from the sun. He eats the cherries one by one as he walks. Over his shoulder he carries a large brown sack the size of a man, filled with rocks and sand. It is his training bag. He walks deep into the forest and finds a tall, strong tree. He ties a rope around the bag and hangs it from a thick branch. On the bag he draws an outline of a person.

After closing his eyes and listening to the wind gust gracefully through the bushes, grass and bright green summer leaves, he opens his eyes and starts to train. He plows the bag many times with varying strikes without restraint, without hesitation and without getting exhausted. Each attack from his feet, elbows, fingers, palm and fists are direct hits to vulnerable spots on a person's body, for these spots affect a person's muscle function, 筋肉系 (the muscular system).

After an hour, he stops hitting the bag. As the bag still swings from right to left, Asoya takes out his *tanto*, which is a dagger, jumps into the air and severs the rope connecting it to the tree with a single swing. The heavy sack hits the ground before Asoya's feet do. Carrying the sack over his shoulder, he heads back to his place of dwelling. Ninja are taught to always be aware; to never be the ones intruded upon, but to be the intruders themselves. Because of this, Asoya is not caught off guard...he stops walking, knowing he is not alone.

"Be gone...all of you, before I give you something you've never been given before," he says as he continues walking.

Seven men come out from behind different trees, each one holding a knife. They are pillagers, robbers. They all laugh hard at Asoya. He stops walking. He drops the sack that is over his shoulder, filled with heavy rocks and sand. It hits the ground hard. He slowly turns around to see all seven of the robbers.

One shouts with aggression for him to give them all of his valuable possessions. The way of those called ninja is to slay, thrashing anyone who is before them. Asoya is ready to slay, ready to thrash and demolish them all using throwing stars. He looks at all of them, searching for vital points on their bodies where his stars can be aimed and land.

"I did give you all a chance to leave…now it is too late," he says as his frown deepens and courses across his face. "It's been a while since I've had to do this, but you all will make for good practice," he says, reaching to his side slowly.

Then he quickly grabs a scroll, unrolls it and starts to read to the seven robbers.

"Remember ye not the former things, neither consider the things of old. Behold, I will do a new thing…" (Isa. 43:18-19)

Asoya's first response is to lay hold upon his throwing stars and hit all seven of them with one, but he does not, knowing that his new Master, Jesus, will not be pleased by such acts. Thus, he grabs a scroll in its place. The robbers look at each other, not knowing what to do. Asoya continues speaking.

"The Lord desires to do a new thing in each of you, in all of you. He desires to make your spirits new and give you a new way of living, and in this new way you no longer have to steal from others, but will help them instead. As it is written, 'Let him that stole steal no more: but rather let him labour, working with *his* hands the thing which is good, that he may have to give to him that needeth.'" (Eph. 4:28)

They all try to take in what Asoya is saying. One of the robbers, whose name is Hiroto, drops his knife, knowing he was raised better. Not all do so, for one of the pillagers is tired of listening and wants to rob Asoya of his possessions by force, despite the words he has just read. This robber's name is Takahiro.

Takahiro whirls his knife around his fingers as he walks intently toward Asoya. Without fear, Asoya takes out a throwing star and spins it toward Takahiro. The star rams into the knife in the man's hand, bashing it from his grip. His knife sparks. He stops walking, holding his hand, for his hand stings. Not because he is cut, he isn't cut at all, but the stinging is from the force of the throw when Asoya threw the star at Takahiro's knife. He looks down at his weapon that is now on the ground and would reach for it, but sees the throwing star lying beside it. In that moment, he knows who Asoya is…

"He is **ninja**!" Takahiro shouts as fright overtakes him.

All of the robbers with him tremble. The season of netsu, 夏の暑さ the summer's heat causes them to sweat, but their panic makes them sweat yet the more.

"An assassin? Me? Humph…not anymore," Asoya says to the seven men.

They are too scared to move, knowing how ninja operate. Once you see a ninja, you disappear. Asoya starts to tell them about how the God of Heaven had made him a different person, a light, a candle. He reads the verses a second time.

"'Remember ye not the former (*past*) things neither consider the things of old (*how you use to do things*). Behold, I will do a new thing…' (Isa. 43:18-19) Allow the God of Heaven to make you new as He has done me," he says as his frown leaves and a faint smile comes across his face.

If an assassin could be labeled a gladiator, Asoya would be named amongst them. He is a ninja who was feared in his own clan. He was unrivaled. After finding out the truth about who he was really doing work for, the great dragon also known in scripture as the devil, he abandoned his creed as an assassin to follow after the words of truth.

This truth that he now follows can only be found in Yeshua Messiah, as known in Hebrew עושי דלמה, or Jesus Christ in today's tongue, the Son of the Living God who was the Savior of all people, even the people who resided in and were from the land of Japan. Asoya is on the path of those who are titled Word Carriers, individuals who are lights and carry God's word to the people around them and throughout their region. This is where Asoya's journey and story continue to be told.

There is a long pause. Asoya looks at each of them, looking them all in their eyes. He takes his eyes off of them briefly to roll up his scroll. As he rolls up the scroll in his hand, all of the seven robbers run, stumbling over themselves getting away from that area. Asoya chuckles as he turns around. Going back over to his large training bag, he lifts it up, draping it over his shoulder.

"Some cold spring water sounds refreshing right now," he says, heading back to his place of residence.

トレーニングセッション

影から
ろうそくに

*Do not
remember the
former (or past)
things, neither
consider the
things of old
(the way things
use to be).
Behold, I will
do a new
thing...*

(Isaiah 43:18-19)

短剣

Mr. Yutaka and the Bookie

There is a man named Mr. Yutaka who owes a bookie a certain amount of money. He borrowed money to take care of his family but is unable to repay the bookie the amount he borrowed at the appointed time. So the bookie sends two men after Mr. Yutaka to take care of him. Their names are Shizu and Leiko. They find Mr. Yutaka leaving the marketplace, corner him on his way back home in an abandoned area, and tell him to pay.

Mr. Yutaka pleads with them both, saying, "Please, give me one more month and I will repay what I owe…I… I don't have the money right now…"

"Hey, Leiko…he says that he can't repay us right now."

"Well, we'll just have to show him what happens to those who can't pay us now, don't we?" Leiko replies, and laughs.

Mr. Yutaka backs up fretfully until his back is against a door of an abandoned building.

"No...please...I..." Mr. Yutaka says, trembling, as Shizu and Leiko draw closer and closer to him, cracking their knuckles while laughing.

He is cornered. They punch Mr. Yutaka. He flies through the old, brittle door, and in the shadows and limited light Leiko and Shizu are visible, standing tall in the doorway, laughing. Mr. Yutaka reaches his shaking hand out, then passes out.

"Now that wasn't nice," a man says.

The two men instantly turn around, surprised that someone is watching. "Who are you?"

"Me?" Asoya asks with his thumb pointing toward his chest. "I'm just a traveler, traveling from place to place, carrying some Good News."

"Wha...Good News?" Shizu asks, not understanding his words.

"Yeah, you might want to take a couple of minutes out of your busy schedule to hear it, that is, if it's not too much for you."

"Now you listen here..."

Asoya interrupts Leiko. "The Good News is that God sent His Son to—"

"The only good news that I have for you is my fist hitting your face!" Leiko says, as he cracks his knuckles.

"He, he, he," Shizu laughs.

"Wow, I wasn't expecting that. At least allow me to finish speaking on the Good News before saying such things," Asoya says, looking at both of them.

"You hear that Shizu? He wasn't expecting that," Leiko mocks. He then reaches into his pocket and pulls out a pair of brass knuckles and puts them on.

"I try to bring you Good News and this is how you treat me?" Asoya asks with a smirk on his face, and then closes his eyes.

Shizu, still laughing, unwraps a chain from around himself and begins to twirl it. Leiko launches at Asoya instantly to strike him with his brass knuckles. Asoya steps slightly to the left, tosses the sword he is carrying in the air, then elbows Leiko in his ribs. Leiko stops in his tracks as though he is paralyzed, then starts to shake.

"What?" Shizu asks, then angrily tries to hit Asoya with his chain, but misses. He swings the chain a second time at Asoya,

Asoya takes out his dagger and swings it hard at the chain to deflect it. The metal chain rings as it comes in contact with his dagger. Asoya puts his weapon away, then looks at Shizu.

In fury, Shizu wraps his chain around his fist and runs at Asoya to punch him. But Asoya steps slightly to the right and chops Shizu on his neck, hitting a nerve and muscle called the Sternocleidomastoid 胸鎖乳突筋. This causes his body to stop and shake. Leiko is on Asoya's left, and Shizu is on his right, still standing and shaking. Asoya puts one hand in the air and catches his sheathed sword that he tossed up before he was charged. Upon catching it, he throws it over his shoulder as though it were a backpack, holding it by a string.

Then he looks at Shizu and Leiko and asks, "Now was all that necessary?"

He takes one step forward, his back now facing Leiko and Shizu. When Asoya steps forward, Leiko and Shizu both crash to the ground, unconscious. He then looks in the direction where Mr. Yutaka had been hit through the door.

*Hmmm…*Asoya thinks, after seeing where Mr. Yutaka is. Asoya then turns back around and kneels before Shizu, takes out a piece of paper, writes on it, then places it upon Shizu's chest.

The note reads:

Shadows are a form of darkness, and that is what you are in. I too was once that way but have chosen not to remain in that state. Darkness is something we are all born into, but God sent us a light…all of the dark deeds that you have ever committed have been paid for by the light that He sent, and this light's name is Jesus. Believe and accept what He has done for you. Jesus the Light has great love for you.

He does the same thing for Leiko, except he places the piece of paper in Leiko's hand, then places a scroll with God's word written upon it on his chest. Asoya then stands upright.

"Whoa…Awesome!" a young voice says from behind him.

"Huh?" Asoya says immediately upon hearing those words. He turns around, only to see a small boy with his eyes fixed upon him,

"That was cool Mister. How'd you do that?"

"Little boy, where's your mother?"

あなたの母はどこですか？

Little boy, what are you doing here....where's your mother?

好奇心が強い

16

"Umm…" the young boy says, thinking, as he looks down at his own feet.

Asoya then hears a voice crying out for help, which is Mr. Yutaka.

"Ahhh…" Mr. Yutaka says in pain. "Help me…somebody please help me."

Asoya looks at the little boy and says, "Go back to where you came from, your mother's probably worried about you."

After that, Asoya turns and aids Mr. Yutaka. Upon entering the building, Asoya moves the wood covering Mr. Yutaka, which came from the brittle door. Then he helps him to his feet.

"Are you okay?"

"Yeah, but…wha…what happened?" Mr. Yutaka asks, still in a daze from being attacked by the two bookies.

"Who? Them?" Asoya turns around and looks at the two men who attacked Mr. Yutaka. "Don't be bothered by them, they will not harm you. Here." Asoya takes out some money from his pouch and hands it to Mr. Yutaka.

"No…I…"

"Just take it," Asoya says gently and with a smile.

Mr. Yutaka relaxes and reaches his hands out. "Thank you… ah, who are you?"

"My name is Asoya, but don't thank me, thank the Lord."

Mr. Yutaka thinks for a moment then asks, "The Lord?"

"Yes, the Lord. I was on my way to share the Good News of His word with the people a few miles from here when I heard commotion as I traveled. It was because of His word I came over here, and from the looks of it, it looks like just in time," Asoya says with a smile, as he puts one hand on Mr. Yutaka's shoulder. "The money you are holding in your hand is a free gift, you owe me nothing…but go and pay the man you owe, and with the money remaining, use it for your family."

Mr. Yutaka's eyes begin to fill with tears. "But you…"

"Hey, it's okay, I have plenty. Just like the money that was given to you was free, so is the Gift of Eternal Life," Asoya says, still smiling. Then he begins to tell Mr. Yutaka about Jesus, and how Jesus paid the price so that everyone else who believed in the name of Jesus could have life and live eternally with Him. Mr. Yutaka receives Jesus in his heart and goes his way rejoicing.

Elisa

"Wow, Mister, you know a lot about a lot of stuff!"

"Huh? You're still here…what are you doing out here by yourself?" Asoya asks, looking down at the boy sternly.

"Well, you see I was playing and…"

"Geto…Geto…" (G-toe, Geto) a young woman cries out.

"Ah-ooo…" the boy says, looking down as though he were in trouble.

"G-toe? That must be your name," he says, looking down at the young boy.

"Geto!" the young woman says as she finds him, but freezes with fear, seeing the two men lying on the ground unconscious and Asoya standing nearby.

"Please Mister, don't hurt the boy…" the woman says with panic in her voice. "I…"

Before she is able to finish, Asoya interjects, "Don't be alarmed, I'm just…"

"You should have seen him, he was cool!" Geto says, jumping up and down.

Asoya calms the young woman down by explaining to her what took place and why the two men were lying on the ground.

"I see," she says as she kneels down, hugs the little boy, then kisses him on the cheek.

"You must be the little boy's mother."

"No, Mister, she's not my mother, well, she's like my mother… are you my mother? Well whatever you are, I'm glad that you take care of me."

She pats Geto on the head. "You can say I'm like his mother. I work at an orphanage home. I was taking the children out for a walk when Geto got away. I made it all the way back home before realizing that he was no longer with us, so…I came looking for him."

"Sorry…" Geto says with his head down.

"It's okay, I'm happy to see that no harm has come to you…I prayed and see, my prayers were answered, God was protecting you."

"God?" Asoya asks raising his eyebrows. "So you know the Lord, the Creator of heaven and earth?"

"Do you?" the woman asks as she takes her eyes off of Geto and fixes them on Asoya. She lifts up her head slightly, as if she were trying to read him.

"I do, I'm actually carrying His word to the people."

"Oh, that's wonderful!" she says with joy. "It's been a long time since I've seen an actual Carrier of God's Word. It's nice to meet you...my name is Elisa, Elisa Hanakotoba. Your name must be...The Word Carrier?" she asks as she bows her head to him, showing respect.

"Ah, Asoya, my name is Asoya," he replies as he bows back to receive her welcome.

"It's nice to meet you, Asoya, you must be the Word Carrier everyone is talking so much about. I couldn't help but notice your fancy sword, it must be valuable to you."

"It's a long story," Asoya says as he gazes upon the ground, as though writing is upon it.

"That is wonderful! The children and I would love to hear your story. Why don't you come by the orphanage and share it with us? The children would love the company and it's always good to hear how God has brought us as far as He has."

"Humph. My story is not meant for the ears of children!" Asoya says, rigidly and austerely.

"Well, that's okay, I'm sure that you have many other stories that you could tell," she says with a smile. "We would love to hear them."

What's wrong with this woman...why is she so welcoming? Asoya thinks.

The summer wind picks up lightly; the sunlight hits the land just right, causing the grass, the hills, the bushes and the cherry blossom trees in the distance to look like an art canvas that has just been freshly painted. The wind lifts a few cherry blossom petals and carries them over to where Asoya is. He watches the petals pass him.

"Okay, but only for a little while," Asoya says, frowning, but in a calm tone.

"Yay!" Geto says excitedly. "Hey Mister, are you going to show me some of your fighting moves?"

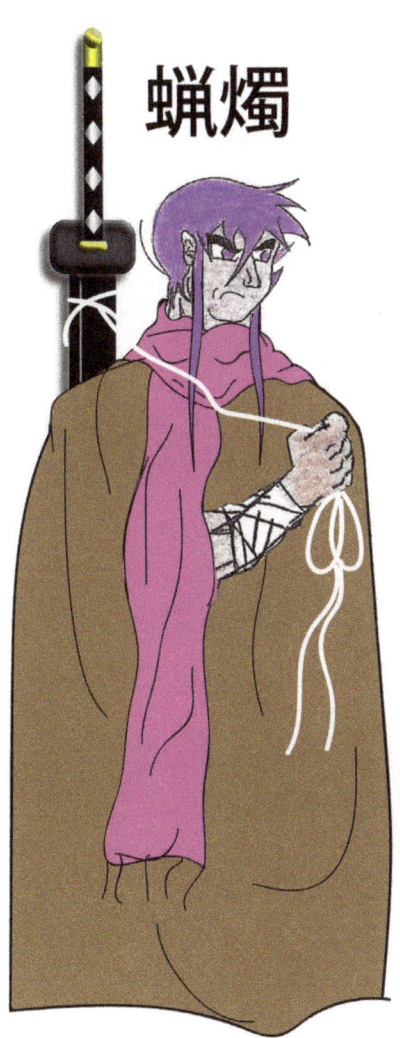

蝋燭

に向かって
孤児院
エリサと

Elisa

優しい
落ち着いた
優しい女性

孤児

Orphan

Train up a child
in the way he
should go: and
when he is old,
he will not
depart from it.

(Proverbs 22:6)

Asoya's Trip to the Orphanage

Elisa, Geto and Asoya start their journey to the orphanage. As they approach their destination Asoya starts to second-guess his decision to speak with the children, but seeing the joyful expression on Geto's face, he presses on. As they arrived, Elisa and the other workers gather all of the children to meet Asoya.

After they sit them down, Elisa says, "Everyone, this is Asoya, say 'hi, Asoya.'"

"Hi, Asoya!" the children all say in unison.

"It's Mr. Asoya…Mister!" Geto shouts, looking at the children, then folds his arms.

"Asoya is a Word Carrier and he has come to share some of his stories with us," she says, looking at all the children, who all have their eyes fixed on Asoya.

Asoya squeezes his sword that is in his hand, then says in anger, "Only a couple."

Seeing the expressions on the children's faces and how ready they are to hear him speak, he softens his tone, then sits down. He places his blade in front of him and begins to share some of God's word with them. As Asoya finishes speaking, he rise up and the children all run in separate directions to play. But one young girl stays behind and just stares at Asoya.

Seeing the young girl's eyes fixed on him, Asoya says, "Little girl, what are you looking"

Before he can finish his question, the girl runs up to him, squeezes both of his legs, and looks up at his face. "I'm glad that you came," she says with a smile. "Please come back and tell us some more stories." She then releases his legs and runs to play with the other children.

Elisa, seeing all of this transpire, smiles then walks over to Asoya and says, "See, that wasn't so bad."

After leaving the orphanage, Asoya goes to a secluded area to practice his swordplay. After swinging his blade a couple of times at the air and slicing through a few rocks, he sheaths his weapon. He takes a deep breath, then holds his sword close to his chest as he looks at the clouds rolling by. The wind is warm but pleasant.

"Lord, You are my Master now, not the clan…why did You allow the Word Carrier before me to make the sacrifice that he did? If he were here, he would be the one telling the people about Jesus right now, not me," Asoya says as he unsheaths his sword and looks down at it.

The Word Carrier before him was the one who revealed the truth of God's word to him. He slowly slides the sword back into its sheath and ties string around the handle of the sheath so he will not draw it out. After some time, he ties his sword to his back, then begins to strike his training bag filled with rocks and sand, until the moon's glow is cast in the night's sky.

Asoya Rejected By the Town's People

As best as Asoya can, he tries to allow the Lord to direct his steps (Proverbs 3:6). He travels to a small village. The village is a small community, but large enough for him to maneuver through. He walks the village, studying the area, and looking for quick escape routes in case he needs to make a swift escape. He takes out some drawing utensils and draws a small map of the village. He is in town for four days and is ready to leave. He prays and seeks the Lord on what he should do next. He allows the word he is carrying to lead him and not his emotions. Rather than leaving the town as he desires, he stays, knowing that is what the Lord wants him to do.

The next day, Asoya sees a family walking together, a man, woman and their child. He approaches them and starts to talk to them about the Lord. They listen. As he continues to speak, others overhear his words and start to gather around; more people come until he is speaking to a crowd. Two men in the crowd get rowdy and start to speak out against Asoya. As the two men cause their disruption, many of the people stop listening to Asoya and give heed to them and join in their ranting,

But he ignores them, continuing to talk about the kingdom of God. One of the men gets past the crowd, then in front of his face. But he ignores him and continues to speak. The man gets angry because he feels Asoya is not taking him seriously, so he raises his hand against him to strike him. Asoya sweeps the man's feet from under him. The man falls backwards to the ground. Asoya then pulls back his fist, frowns and punches at the man's face…his punch stops an inch from the man's face,

"Here's some wisdom for you: you should not attack the one who you know nothing about," Asoya says with sternness.

The man looks at Asoya's knuckles, then back at Asoya, His glare can be seen from behind his fist. Another man picks up a stone and throws it at Asoya. He catches it, then turns, looking at the man who threw it.

"I wouldn't do that if I were you," Asoya says, issuing a warning.

The man picks up an even larger stone and casts it at Asoya. He shatters the stone with his fist. Powder from the crushed rock falls to the ground.

拒絶

Rejection

拳粉々石

私は彼に伝えようとしました！

"That…that was a solid stone…" the second man says with fear as he starts to tremble.

Asoya says, "If I did this to a stone, imagine what would have happened if this fist plowed into your face."

The second man stands there, still trembling, looking at the shattered stone and the dust that is still rising off of Asoya's fist.

"Mercy," Asoya says as he laughs, remembering the words of the Word Carrier before him. "Blessed are the merciful for they shall obtain mercy…remember how you were shown mercy this day," he says as he turns and walks away.

When he is a distance away from the people, he turns and looks in their direction.

"Tough crowd…this must have been what Noah felt like when he tried to warn the people that it was going to rain, flooding the earth as it is written in the scrolls of Genesis, the book of beginnings, and they didn't listen."

He walks back to the inn he is staying in to gather his things. Asoya is ready to leave, but is told through the word he is reading to stay, so he stays.

Sin and Shadows

The next day, Asoya leaves the inn and goes back into town to get some food. It is early in the morning. The temperature has dropped, the air is cold and there is a faint fog. When he reaches the town, the sun has already come out. He passes a man sitting outside on a stool playing a *shakuhachi*.

The *shakuhachi* is a Japanese flute made out of bamboo. Asoya stops and listens. The melody is peaceful. He continues to walk. Asoya sees an elderly woman raking leaves from around her shop.

He approaches her and asks, "Are you open?"

"Sure, come right on in," she replies with a smile.

He picks up three peaches and two *chimaki*, traditional dumplings that are steamed. He pays the woman. As he hands her the money, a man walks up to him.

"Hey…" the man says.

Asoya looks at the man out of the corner of his eye, then frowns. "What do you seek?"

"Aren't you that Word Bringer or something who spoke to us last night?" he asks.

Asoya replies, "Yes, I am bringer of The Word…"

"Those were some amazing moves, your moves were the moves of a true warrior."

"Warrior?" Asoya asks, looking down at the man who is marveling at him.

The man continues. "You said some pretty interesting things last night. Things about a Savior, and things about the past, how God wants to do a new thing in all of us. I never heard such words before."

Asoya relaxes, knowing the man is there to hear the Word he is carrying. A restaurant is nearby. He asks if the man wants to hear the word over a meal, and he agrees. They enter the restaurant and take a seat. After ordering some food, Asoya speaks many things concerning the word to the man.

"Sin is like a shadow that has been cast upon our lives. It follows us everywhere we go…in order for this shadow to dissipate, light must first shine on it. Jesus is that light, and those who receive Him—"

"You're still here in this town?"

Asoya turns and sees who is speaking to him. He recognizes his face. It is the man he tripped the previous night for attempting to strike him.

"You again. So you decided to come and listen to these words that I am carrying."

The man picks up a big fish from a customer's table, then smacks Asoya across the side of his face with it.

Asoya sighs as he turns his head and says, "Why don't you hit the other side of my face…just to make it even?"

Smack!

The man hits Asoya on the other side of his face with even more force. (Matthew 5:39)

"Are you done?" he asks, looking up at the man who has just used a fish as a weapon against him. The man continues to frown at Asoya. "Good, have a seat."

The man tosses the fish aside, then sits down.

"Have some red leaf tea," Asoya says, as he pours the man a cup. Steam lifts off of the cup. "I was telling him that sin is like a shadow that has been cast over our lives."

The man clears the table with his arm in anger, Asoya's plate and the plate of the man who is sitting with him, along with their cups, smash on the floor. Asoya grabs hold of his blade, bringing it from around his shoulder. He looks down at it, seeing that it is tied shut. He remembers that he tied his sword handle to the sheath so he will not use it.

"How dare you bring these teachings to our town!" the man shouts.

Everyone inside the restaurant, including the restaurant owner, all fix their eyes on Asoya. He stares intensely at his sheathed sword. Before the man can speak again, Asoya gets up and signals for the man to take it outside of the restaurant. He walks outside. The man follows him. Asoya stops walking and turns around to face the man who has caused a ruckus in the restaurant.

The Nine Paid Assailants

"**N**o need to cause a scene, you have my attention. I didn't come to this town to fight anyone...only to speak. If your desire is not to hear, then that is you, but do not disturb those who do," Asoya says with conviction.

"You embarrassed me in front of the entire community!" the man shouts in frustration.

After staring at the man for a moment, Asoya sighs, softens his face then responds. "I did no such thing. You embarrassed yourself by attempting to harm me." He then reaches up and touches his own face. "You even spanked my face twice with a fish." (John 18:23)

The man giggles but Asoya does not.

"Now, I've come to embarrass you," the man says with boldness.

"Embarrass me...that...doesn't sound very beneficial to me..."

The man walks up to Asoya, raising his hand against him to hit him. Asoya catches his hand.

"I said this to you before, and I will say it again...I wouldn't... do that...if I...were you." He releases the man's hand and says, "A second time mercy has been shown to you." He turns to walk off but stops because nine other men are nearly at their location. "And who are they?"

"Them? Ha ha, just people I paid to embarrass you."

The nine men make it to their location.

"So…you actually paid these men to attack me? That's…actually pretty mean, once you think about it. Shouldn't you be nice to new people who enter into your village?"

All ten of them laugh as they look at each other, then back at Asoya.

He closes his hands to make fists and says, "Leave…"

One of the nine men takes out a pair of nunchaku to demonstrate his skill to Asoya.

"Nunchakus? You're coming at me with nun-chucks?"

Another man casts a rock at Asoya.

He catches it with his hand and says, "Listen…"

Before he can finish his sentence, the man with the nunchakus gets close enough to him to strike him with his nun-chucks, hitting Asoya in the face, chest and his shoulder blade. Asoya staggers back-wards and shakes his head.

"Wow, I did not…see that coming, I was trained in the arts of shadow combat. You're better than I thought you were."

The other eight men back up and get in position, taking out their weapons randomly.

"I wouldn't do that if I were you…"

They all laugh, ignoring Asoya's words, for they feel he is not as skilled as the townspeople say, due to him being struck several times with the nunchakus.

"But since you insist...watch this..." Asoya throws the rock in the air.

They all look up at it. As they are looking up, Asoya runs up the building wall and does a back flip. When he lands he spin kicks two of the men in the face, then trips a third. The fourth, fifth and sixed men he hits with a single move. They hit the ground. Asoya rises and holds out his hand. The rock lands in the center of his palm. The seventh attacker takes out a knife and throws it at Asoya; Asoya takes out a throwing star and casts it at the knife.

His star is flung harder, knocking the knife off course. The knife hits the dirt and spins a few times before coming to a complete halt. By that time the seventh paid attacker runs at Asoya, swinging a thick stick. Asoya block the stick with his hand, breaks it in two, then spin kicks him in the jaw. The man twirls twice on the tips of his toes before collapsing. The eighth and ninth assailants run at Asoya at the same time. He takes one step back. The two men hit each other, then fall, but though they fall they are not unconscious.

"Stay on the ground, it is far too hot to be doing this today," he says, looking down at the two men.

There are no clouds covering the sun, so its rays are beaming down on them. One of the aggressors that just fell on the ground listens, pretending to be asleep and sucking his thumb, but the other one insists upon fighting. This man's name is Fumihiro. He is the strongest out of the bunch, a blacksmith by trade, making and repairing anything that has to do with metal. Fumihiro reaches for his spiked stick as he rises.

He does not realize that Asoya is well trained for such occasions in the arts of combat and the shadows. Asoya grabs his sword's handle, ready to extract it to halt his attacker where he stands, but stops because of it being tied to his sheath. He grunts.

"Remember ye not the former things (*the way things use to be*), neither consider the things of old (*Things from the past*)," (Isa. 43:18) he says as he tosses his sheathed sword to the side. He remembers why it is tied yet again, and takes out his dagger, waiting for Fumihiro to reach him.

Fumihiro swings the clubbed stick. Asoya slices the top end of the stick where the spikes are. His dagger cuts through it as though it is a mere piece of freshly baked bread. The top end of the stick plummets to the ground. Asoya puts his dagger away, then grabs the man by the shoulder with one hand and with the other he digs his elbow deep on the man's deltoid muscle, located on his shoulder 三角筋.

Fumihiro releases his hold on the stick. When the stick hits the ground, Asoya kicks it, then taps him twice on his pectoral major muscle 大胸筋 using his thumb on the right side of the man's chest. Fumihiro starts to stagger and wobble from side to side as he walks past Asoya. Once he passes Asoya, he collapses to lie stretched out on the hot ground.

"I am a light…that is the **only** reason you found me! I did not hide in the shadows as I was taught to do. My new Master tells me that I am a light, so that is what I am," Asoya says, looking down at Fumihiro, who is snoring with his mouth wide open.

A bug flies in Fumihiro's mouth. Asoya chuckles, then looks at the rest of the fallen mob.

"Those who are lights, we are like cities; a city that is set on a hill **cannot** be hidden," he says as he walks over to his sheathed sword and picks it up off the ground. "Hidden," he says, looking over at one of the buildings that is casting a shadow. He gazes at the shadow. "The Lord is doing a new thing in me. A new thing."

Asoya looks at his sheathed blade, knowing that it is because of God's word that he does not draw it out and use it on those men. He grips it tightly, wanting to draw it out.

"Now it's just you," he says, pointing his finger at the man who smacked him across the face with the fish. "Will you listen to these words now?" he asks. He takes out one of the scrolls and starts to read from it, talking to the man about Christ. He reads the entire first chapter of the gospel of John.

Asoya finishes. "Now you've heard the word, you can't say you didn't hear. Peace be unto you." He walks off, then stops and turns, looking at the man. "A third time you have been shown mercy, now go and show that same mercy to someone else as it was shown to you this day."

"Mercy…" the man says, looking at the other men who are lying on the ground. "What are you, a Ronin…a Samurai? If you are, please do not bring the wrath of your shogun upon me," he says, frightened upon thinking on the words that Asoya spoke concerning being shown mercy a third time.

"My shogun…why does everyone think I am Samurai? I am no Samurai, and I am far from a Ronin…I have a Master and His name is Jesus. He is in heaven, seated at the right hand of the Father. God wants to be your Father too…but if you must give me a title, though I am not worthy of one, let it be this…a Word Carrier."

Asoya turns and walks, leaving the man's presence. The man stands there, comprehending that Asoya could have caused him bodily harm, but instead chose to show him mercy and spoke to him about Christ the Savior who came into the world. He turns and looks at Asoya who is making his way back into the restaurant.

"A …Word Carrier…" he says to himself as he looks at the nine men who are starting to groan on the ground as they wake up. One still pretends to be asleep, not knowing that Asoya is no longer there.

"Now that's never happened to me before," Asoya says. "He actually hit me in the face…with a fish. I thought fish were meant to be eaten, not smacking faces."

Asoya makes his way back to the restaurant. He hears the sound of the flute still being played. It calms him. Asoya pays for all of the damages the man caused and apologizes to the owner of the restaurant for the disruption.

慈悲を示す

Show Mercy

You be therefore merciful, as your (*heavenly*) Father also is merciful. (Luke 6:36)

Blessed are the merciful: for they shall obtain (*be shown*) mercy. (Matthew 5:7)

Asoya Drops a Large Bag of Food Off at the Orphanage

soya carries a large sack of food to the orphanage. He looks around vigilantly to make sure no one sees him, then sets the bag down close to the front door softly, making sure the food inside of the bag does not shift or cause a sudden noise that would alert the people at the orphanage of his presence. He starts to leave. The door opens gently. Elisa looks down at the bag of food and smiles. She sees Asoya.

"Hey," she says, trying to get his attention.

Asoya stops, still facing the direction he is walking in.

"It's good to see you," she says, happy to see Asoya. He is silent. "I figured it was you who has been leaving food here for this orphanage… thank you."

"You're welcome," he says as he continues to walk forward.

"Don't go."

Asoya stops, with his back facing Elisa. "I apologize, but I must go."

"The least you can do is let me cook a meal for you to say thank you for the many meals we've been able to eat here because of you. Just one meal, and you can leave. I know that you're hungry from your many travels."

Asoya takes his sword from his shoulder and holds it in his hand. He watches the summer wind dance through the trees. The trees sway slowly from side to side. He sighs, turns his head in Elisa's direction, and nods. They enter the orphanage.

"Interesting artwork," Asoya says as he looks around, seeing painted pictures on the walls inside of the orphanage.

"Thank you, I did them myself. I really like to paint." She smiles as she looks around at her artwork.

She tells Asoya to have a seat at the table as she heads into the kitchen and starts to cook. Elisa cuts up enoki mushrooms and shiitake mushrooms and placed them in a broth. It starts to boil as she adds other vegetables to the soup.

"And those?" he asks, pointing to the room that is behind Elisa.

She turns and looks into the room.

"O no…" She covers her mouth, attempting not to laugh. "The children did those."

The smells of soy and chicken broth fill the room as she prepares the soup. When she is finished cooking, she sets down a bowl of soup in front of Asoya along with a cup of water and a second bowl filled with rice. Asoya looks down at his bowl of mushroom soup.

45

He doesn't blink for a long period of time. Elisa notices his silence and fixed gaze.

"Asoya…are you all right?"

Asoya continues to look down at his soup.

"Asoya…"

"Huh?" he says as he lifts up his head, looking at Elisa.

"Is everything all right? Do you see a problem with the soup?"

"No," Asoya says softly, as he picks up his soup spoon.

"What is it?"

"I am trying to figure out how the Word Carrier dealt with those who rejected his words, even attempts to attack him while speaking the words of truth."

"Attackers…were you attacked?"

"I was."

"Are you hurt…are you all right?" she asks with tears in her eyes.

Asoya smiles slowly.

"They prevailed not against me. If I had not remembered the words of the Word Carrier, they surely would have been broken… permanently," Asoya says as he balls up his fist. He looks at Elisa, then relaxes his hand.

"I know it's not easy being rejected, especially if you're trying to help people. I remember being told what Jesus said about rejection and it stayed with me. He said 'Whoever listens to you listens to me; whoever rejects you rejects me; but whoever rejects me rejects him who sent me,'" (Luke 10:16) she says, looking at Asoya's hands. Then she looks up at his face.

"Whoever listens to you...listens to me," he says, looking down at his fists.

He sips some of the mushroom soup while Elisa continues to explain.

"That means if they're listening to you and what you're saying about the word, then they're listening to Him, but if they're not listening to you then they're not listening to Him, because you are speaking His word. You are speaking to them on His behalf."

On His behalf? That sounds just like what the Word Carrier before me said when I was listening to him speak God's word to the people... he said he was Christ's representative on the earth. So I'm speaking on Christ's behalf, he thinks as he continues to listen.

"If they reject you...it's not really you they are rejecting, Asoya, but they are rejecting Him."

Asoya is amazed by her answer. That is just what he needs to hear. He grins as he finishes up his mushroom soup.

"Are you sure you're not a Word Carrier, Elisa?" he asks, as he places the empty bowl down on the table gently.

"I believe that everyone who believes on Jesus is a mouthpiece to be used by Him, but there are those who are specially set aside to do His work," she says.

Asoya finishes his water, thanks her for the meal, then heads out the door.

Asoya and the Word Carrier
Before Him

After Asoya's seventh visit to the orphanage in a span of five months, he feels comfortable enough with Elisa to tell her his story.

"I was once an orphan myself," he says as he sits down on the carpet, crosses his legs, then props his encased sword against his chest.

"Really?" Elisa asks with amazement.

"No one cared for me when I was an orphan. I was on my own. That's when I was taken in by a clan, I became a ninja of the highest ranking."

"That's why you carry that sword. To…remind you where you came from," Elisa says as she begins to understand.

"I was given an assignment to take out a threat who was opposing the plans of my master. But on this mission …I encountered something I had never seen before. This was no ordinary target, this target had protection far beyond anything I had ever encountered.

It was an angel protecting him. I did not know that at the time, I just knew that this being was massive."

"Wow, this is quite a story," she says, intrigued by his words.

"Our weapons were no match against him."

"So, this target was protected by an angel? Who was this target?"

"A Word Carrier."

"A Word Carrier?" Elisa asks in amazement at his reply.

"At the time I knew not what a Word Carrier was. My men and I were forced to retreat, we were unable to apprehend the target. I was curious to why our forces were no match against his, so I returned to his home secretly, without permission from my master, and what I found I understood not. A man who was peaceful, joyful…happy, who was nice to me even after he found out I was trying to take his life. He talked about Jesus as though He were right there. I believed in the darkness…but he stood for the light," Asoya says as he gazes into the distance.

"What happened to him?"

"My master found out that I was meeting with the Word Carrier regularly. My clan came after me for consulting with the enemy. This Word Carrier sacrificed his life to save mine," Asoya says as he rises, turns his back to Elisa, throws his sword over his shoulder, then walks out the front door into the darkness, for it is night.

Elisa rushes to the front door and yells, "You are welcome to come back any time!" Her voice echoes as Asoya disappears in the shadows.

過去の反射

Geto

50

Asoya's Followed

Night has emerged and darkness covers the sky like a thick blanket. As Asoya walks on the trail he has taken many times before, he remains in stealth as he goes to his hideout. He hears footsteps treading the dirt in the distance, not just one pair of feet, but multiple. Asoya covers his face with the magenta scarf he has wrapped around his neck in haste, then pulls part of the cloak covering his body over his head, and hides behind a tree.

"I'm being followed," Asoya says as a band of ninjas pass him by. He hides in the shadows unnoticed with his hand on his blade, looking up to the sky.

Recognizing the insignia on their swords, his eyes widen.

"It's my old clan...I thought I was done battling with them. Could it be because I am carrying the word?" he asks himself, as he looks at the scroll he is carrying with God's word written upon it.

He does not leave that spot, but remains there for an hour, for he is waiting for the ninjas to be fully gone from that location. When he knows they are gone, he starts to travel. Asoya is surreptitious, cautious in his movements; practicing the art of quietude 沈黙, he avoids the ninjas' detection.

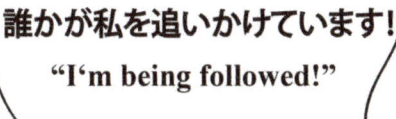
誰かが私を追いかけています！
"I'm being followed!"

追求

"It's my old clan...I thought I was done battling with them."

彼らの
それでも
追いかけて
私

Ruthless Vermillion

The next day after speaking God's word to a few people he passed by while traveling, Asoya rests for a while, then decides to wait until night to cover the land to do more traveling. As he travels he halts his movements, hearing yet again treading of leaves and grass in the distance. He recognizes the sound and pattern of their movements.

"Huh? There…still coming after me?" As he speaks, Asoya puts his hand on his sword, slowly drawing it out of its sheath.

"I want to…but something is telling me not to," he says as he places his blade back within his sheath and releases his hold from the handle. Just as Asoya thinks this, he is surrounded by eight ninjas from his old clan. They flip out of different shadows, their hands on their weapons, ready to extract them.

"Past shadows," Asoya says, squeezing his sheathed sword.

"We finally found you, Ruthless Vermillion," a voice says.

Asoya grins. "Ruthless Vermillion? It's been a while since I've been called by that name. My shadow name…"

Ruthless Vermillion was the name that the clan members titled Asoya due to his brutality when battling.

"But that shadow has long since passed," he says, looking up and seeing the group of ninja.

The one speaking to Asoya is the head ninja who has a small band of soldier ninja with him. "Did you truly think you could escape us?" he asks, as though making fun of him.

"To be honest…yes, I did," Asoya replies with a chuckle.

"Behold the clan's traitor, men. He was the highest ranking. Asoya…can you believe that he alone was awarded a sword that had the words *dragon smoke* ドラゴンスモーク written on its metal? Him!" the head ninja says with mockery and disgust. The ninjas looks at each other, remembering when their master awarded Asoya the sword called *dragon smoke*.

Asoya immediately interjects, "Look at yourselves and who it is that is with you. You have to travel in packs to capture me…but if I were still in the clan, I alone would have been sent after you if you strayed. Remember that. And do not call me by my shadow name, Ruthless Vermillion…if you must give me a title, call me 'A Candle'."

"You dare speak to the head ninja that way?" one of the ninjas shouts in anger as he runs toward Asoya to silence him for insulting the head ninja.

"I understand," Asoya says, watching the ninja draw closer to him. "Mercy is not the way of the clan, but I am not in the clan."

The ninja kicks. Asoya balls up his fist and elbows the ninja on his anklebone, then punches him on the side of his kneecap. He digs four of his fingers in the ninja's right bicep muscle, causing him to drop his sword, then quickly sweeps the ninja's legs from under him. As the ninja falls, Asoya drops his fist on the ninja's chest. The ninja crashes to the ground, back first, then bounces and flips over to his stomach from the force of Asoya's fist. The ninja lies there…unconscious.

"No, but how dare you attack the one who you **do** know something about…" Asoya says forcefully as he looks at the ninja lying on the ground, still breathing.

A second ninja attacks but is unable to overpower Asoya, He kicks the ninja twice; the ninja hits the ground. Asoya glances down at him.

"Mercy," Asoya says, as he takes his eyes of the ninja on the ground and looks at the rest of them, remembering what is written in the scrolls that he now carries.

After witnessing the actions of the one who was once the highest ranking in their clan, one of the ninja says this to the others: "Master sent Gekijō after Asoya to bring him in…and Asoya defeated him."

"What?" another ninja says, amazed. "He defeated Gekijō? Tracker Gekijō?"

"Yes," the ninja affirmed.

Gekijō is also known in the clan as the ninja named Shatter.

"Shatter," Asoya says, loud enough for himself to hear as he thinks about how he tried to warn Shatter, to prevent him falling through the floor when he noticed the wooden floorboards were unstable. Shatter didn't listen.

"Tracker Gekijō was sent to bring Asoya in, but Asoya was the one who brought Gekijō back to the clan, unconscious, over his shoulder, and dropped him before Master."

"Enough!" the head ninja shouts, growing weary of hearing tales of Asoya. "We were ordered to bring in this traitor, so we **will** bring him in!"

"They know not, neither will they understand; they walk on in darkness," Asoya says, speaking Psalm 82:5 as he looks at all the ninjas, as well as thinking about Shatter. He understands why they are doing the things they are doing. Darkness is what ninjas walk in. They do not understand the concept of being a light. Courtesy of the clan and being raised in the shade, they are like shadows, something that reflects their spiritual condition, causing them to react like they do…to react like vultures.

"You were once our best ninja, now you're our highest paid **target,** ha ha!" the head ninja says, but Asoya speaks firmly.

"Hold your words, my life is no longer my own."

"You're right, it now belongs to my blade," the head ninja says, with disappointment at the very sight of Asoya. As he speaks, all six ninjas draw out their swords. Their swords ring, echoing through the trees.

"Humph…I wouldn't do that if I were you."

"You're right, let's fight in the smoke." Just then, one of the six ninjas throws down two smoke bombs.

BOOM!

There is silence, but only briefly. The chiming of metal rings throughout the atmosphere for several minutes. One ninja, in fear, jumps out of the smoke, but Asoya grabs him by the ankle and yanks him back in. When the smoke clears, only Asoya remains standing. The head ninja is squirming on the ground. He takes out a throwing star and throws it at Asoya with the little strength he has left, and it lands in Asoya's leg. Asoya reaches down and grabs hold of the star and pulls it from his outer left thigh. He frowns and grabs hold of his sword handle, ready to draw it out, angered that the ninja hit him with a star.

Asoya's chest sparks orange twice, then starts to glow red. He hits his knees and grabs his chest, holding his heart in pain. Words appear in Hebrew, 'תקידב בל', which being interpreted translates to the words, "Heart Check or Heart Examination." It projects from his chest and appears before his eyes. He straightway understands the Hebrew words but wonders what they mean.

He heard a voice speaking quietly within him that says, "Examine yourself."

"Examine? Why do I need to examine myself?" he asks as he looks at the sword in his hand, still encased within it sheath. He hears the voice again.

"Examine yourself, and see if you are in the faith *or not*...prove (*test or validate*) your own self. Do you not know your own self, how that Christ Jesus is in you, except you be *a* reprobate (*a person who is undisciplined*)?" (2 Cor. 13:5)

His chest then stops glowing and the red words written in Hebrew disappear. He looks down at his chest and sees that the Hebrew writing is gone.

"Must be because of this blade that I am holding and how quick I was to want to draw it out," he says, as he gets off his knees, still holding his chest.

The head ninja passes out. A second ninja is on the ground, squirming, crawling, trying to get away. Asoya walks over to the ninja. He turns and sees Asoya looking down at him. The ninja understands that no one escapes the clutches of the assassin known as Ruthless Vermillion. Fear strikes him, knowing that Asoya is going to take him out. But he does not. He kneels down and places his hand on the ninja's shoulder. After a moment, the ninja relaxes and the fear leaves.

He speaks. "You can't be Ruthless Vermillion, you're not him, are you? For though you fight like him, he is more ruthless and spares no one. But you spare...besides that, you do not have the scars on your body that he does."

"That is because the God that I serve is a healer. He has made me new; even the scars that once covered me are there no longer. He wants to heal you too and make you new."

The ninja pulls his *mask* down and smiles at Asoya, then says, "I would like to be made new...like you." He then passes out.

Asoya places a few scrolls inside of the ninja's shirt, then stands upright. He turns to leave but walks with a limp.

"Huh?" Asoya asks, as he puts his hand upon his forehead. When he brings his hand back down, he notices that it is bloody. "Wow, a ninja as well as the head ninja actually got me, ha ha."

Elisa's Counsel

Asoya makes his way to the orphanage and knocks on the door. Elisa opens the door.

Seeing the blood on Asoya's forehead and leg she asks, "Asoya, what happened to you?"

He tries to think of what to say but stutters, "Ahhhh…"

"Must you always get in trouble?" she asks as she brings a bowl filled with warm water to clean Asoya's wound before bandaging him up.

"I was going to strike eight ninjas tonight with my blade, but something inside of me would not allow me to do so."

"Did you?"

"No, I only disarmed them before knocking them out."

"Asoya, that someone was the Lord."

"The Lord…" Asoya says quietly as he looks at the scroll he is carrying, which has God's word written upon it. He looks down at his chest and holds it. "I'm not cut out to be a Word Carrier, I'm an ex-assassin, the one they called Ruthless Vermillion."

"Oh, but you are cut out for this, Asoya, and you can be used by the Lord." She puts her hand upon his head and says, "Stay strong, Asoya, you were chosen to be a Word Carrier. I believe in you, and God believes in you." Elisa then begins to bandage up his head.

Geto comes into the room, excited to see Asoya. "Hey, Mr. Asoya. Are you going to teach me some moves today?"

"No…not tonight, maybe some other time, Geto," he says as he pats the boy on the head.

"Okay!" he replies enthusiastically.

Four more children surround Elisa and begin to pull on her arms, saying, "Come on, come on!"

"Yeah, come on, Miss Elisa, we have to show you what we made in the mud," Geto says, joining in.

"In the mud? Aren't you children supposed to be sleeping right now?" Elisa asks, looking at all of the joyful expressions on the children's faces.

"Come on, Miss Elisa, please?" Geto says, getting closer to her.

"Okay, okay… 'bye, Asoya," she says joyfully, as she is dragged off by the children.

"'Bye…Elisa."

He sits there, staring at the scroll in his hand. After bandaging his leg, he rises quietly and leaves out of the front and closes the door behind him. Asoya returns to the place where he is staying, which is well hidden. After doing a few pushups, he sits down and begins to ponder on the words that Elisa spoke to him.

"If I am chosen to be a Word Carrier, why am I still dealing with my past, and why do past thoughts haunt me? Am I doing something wrong? Elisa said she believes in me. And that God believes in me. I've been doing things on my own for so long, but…I've come to realize that those who carry God's word are never alone," Asoya says as he lies on his mat on the floor, with his hands behind his head. "Was that You, Lord, who told me not to draw out my blade and to examine myself?" Asoya sits up, then looks at his sword, which has been placed in the corner of his room. He picks up the scroll that is next to his bed. "Hummm…" he says as he looks at the scroll intensely.

The Shadow

As Asoya opens the scroll to meditate on the words that were written therein, he hears a sound outside his window.

Crackle. Crackle. Crackle.

"Huh? That sounds like the rustling of leaves," he says, focusing his hearing. He does not hear any wind but subtle movement. Asoya quickly blows out the candle in his room and grabs his sword from the corner and goes outside silently. The moon is bright, casting many shadows, obscurities. He notices where the moon's light is cast and avoids those spots. Hidden by a shadow, he glances around the corner.

Crackle. Crackle. Crackle.

"It's that noise again. In the exact same spot, it's not scattering to the rest of the trees." Asoya brings his head back around the corner, being assured that it is not the wind. He moves to another shadow. He is able to focus in the direction from which the sound is coming. Seeing a shadowy figure in the trees, he draws closer quietly, unnoticed by the shadowy figure. He see a sheathed sword behind the figure's back.

A ninja, I thought so, he says within himself as he steps into the light. The ninja, seeing that he is no longer hidden, jumps down from the tree but stays in the shadows. The figure gawks at Asoya with a slight tilt to its head, staring.

Unable to see what clan the ninja is from, due to him lurking in the darkness, Asoya asks, "Who sent you?"

The ninja straightens his posture, then tilts his head to the other side, still looking at Asoya without blinking.

Hearing no reply, Asoya asks him a second time, "Who sent you, and what clan do you claim?"

The ninja remains silent…soundless…

"No answer? Humph, well, if you came to hear the word, you have come to the right place…if it is truth you seek."

Unresponsive to the words of Asoya, this mysterious ninja draws out his sword.

Asoya responds by saying, "I wouldn't do that if I were you…"

The ninja points his sword at Asoya and says, "Yes…you would…" He then gets into a stance that indicates he is ready to attack at any moment.

"Now do you speak. Why have you come? Has to be because of the clan."

Asoya notices written on the ninja's sword are the words *dragon smoke*.

"So, you're the new ninja that the master awarded and bestowed that sword upon? Only the assassin with the highest level due to successful solo missions can hold that sword, and it looks like you are him now," he says, intrigued. He watches the ninja closely, for he understands this ninja is not just a mere foot soldier ninja, but one who is highly skilled.

"Ninja, the wielder of the sword hailed as *dragon smoke*, how many have fallen due to you swinging the sharpness of that katana?"

The ninja looks down at his sword, reading the words written in red. He then looks back up at Asoya, shrugs, points his sword at Asoya with one hand, then signals with his other hand for Asoya to come and attack him. A taunt. Asoya squeezes the sheathed sword in his hand, asking the ninja a second time the same question. He remains silent in response to the words of Asoya, as all who are raised in the clan are trained to do: stay mute, remain silent just like a shadow. Thus is the way of path of those that call them-selves ninja.

Without warning, the ninja charges him. Asoya places his hand upon his blade handle, but hears something inside tell him not to.

"Again? Lord, if that is You, why do You not allow me to defend myself?"

Asoya's heart flashes red once again, causing it to glow. He looks down at his chest...'תקידב בל'. The ninja is only seconds away from striking Asoya!

"Lord, forgive me, but...I must!" Right then Asoya draws out his sword.

The ninja swings, and Asoya blocks the thrust of his opponent's sword with his. *BAM!* The force of the ninja's blow colliding with Asoya's sword throws Asoya backward, causing him to roll and slide. When Asoya stops sliding, he looks down at his sword due to it vibrating.

Asoya is breathless and says with astonishment, "What kind of strength is this? Such power..." He touches the back side of the blade, the dull end, to stop it from rattling. He then smirks and says with laughter in his voice, "A-he...it's very apparent that he has not come to hear the Living Word, Ha ha..."

The ninja disappears discreetly into a shadow. Asoya looks around almost in disarray, gripping his sword, searching for the one who has tracked him to that location.

"Huh?" Asoya says as he lifts up his head, only to see that his opponent is above him.

The ninja comes down feet-first. Asoya rolls out of the way, jumps to his feet, and runs toward the ninja. He throws a punch, but the ninja blocks it and then kicks Asoya in his chest, knocking the air out of one of his lungs. The power of his kick causes Asoya to slide backwards, but as he is sliding, catching his breath, Asoya grabs the mask of his opponent to see his face. The ninja is unveiled...the mysterious assassin lifts up his head slowly until Asoya sees his face, but because of the darkness Asoya cannot make out who he is. The ninja then walks out of the shadows to reveal his true form…

"Huh?" Asoya gasps as he looks upon the face of his enemy. "His face…it…looks just like mine, and his hair…he even has the scars that I used to have but was healed from. Is that the *old me*? Ruthless Vermillion, but…how?"

The ninja just stares at him with darkness in his eyes.

Asoya quickly gathers himself, stands to his feet and asks, "Where did you come from? Where?!"

The ninja smiles, sheathing his sword called *dragon smoke*, then takes out a smoke bomb. Asoya runs, but he doesn't run away, he runs to the ninja known as Ruthless Vermillion. He jumps and kicks in the ninja's direction. Without hesitation, the ninja crashes the smoke bomb to the ground. The ground rumbles almost like the sound of thunder. The bomb sparks before erupting. *BOOM!* This smoke bomb is powerful, powerful enough to knock Asoya out of the air…he is flung back and hits the ground. Smoke engulfs the atmosphere.

Coughing, Asoya asks, "Where is he?" He gets up off of his back as he tries to search for him through the smoke. When the smoke disperses, the ninja is unable to be found or seen.

"Vermillion…" he says to himself, trying to figure out how he has just faced a ninja that embodies him and his characteristics to the fullest, from movements all the way down to his scars.

"Ruthless. To slow me down, he knocked the air out of one of my lungs," he says as he grabs his chest where the ninja kicked him.

He searches two hours for the ninja who embodies the Asoya from the clan, the ninja who was known as Ruthless Vermillion… looking in almost all of the shadows in the places that are close to where he is, but Ruthless Vermillion, the holder of the sword called *dragon smoke* is gone. Asoya looks at his blade before placing it in its sheath. He returns to his place of residence mystified. The remainder of the night he stays awake, for sleep has fled from him, due to him thinking on the ninja…the blade…the past, the past Asoya.

The end of *Asoya*: **Shadows from the Past**
(過去からの影): *Section 1*

隠蔽の芸術

許してください、しかし私は自分自身を守らなければなりません!

戦闘
Combat

交戦

**For though we walk in the flesh,
we do not war after the flesh:
(2 Corinthians 10:3)**

Section 2
過去からの影

The Condemnation, the Revelation and the Salvation

非難　　　啓示　　　救い

The Old Nature

The following day, Asoya rises up early and goes to the orphanage home to speak to Elisa.

After he tells her the details of the incident that happened the previous night, she says, "It sounds to me like that attack was just your *old nature* trying to resurface."

"What? My old nature?" Asoya asks, trying to process what he has just heard.

"Yes, your past is trying to *resurrect* itself."

"Resurrect? How can one's past revive itself? Why do you speak such lunacy?"

"It's not lunacy and this is far from madness, Asoya, It's the truth. You are a new creature in Christ Jesus, old things have passed away — *your old self and nature* — but behold, all things have become new."

Asoya is reluctant, adverse to accept what she is speaking, but he listens.

"Apparently your old self, your old nature or the past you, is trying to resurface ...to get you to return to the way you once were.

The ninja called Ruthless Vermillion?" she asks, unsure if she has gotten his shadow name, the name that the clan gave him, correctly.

He nods.

"The name that the clan gave you is the past. That's not who you are. Don't let your past win. You are a new person, that's why you heard that voice on the inside of you that told you not to draw out your blade…because that was your old way of thinking and handling situations that arose. You are Asoya the Candle, Asoya the Word Carrier."

"I see, I am now a Candle…but what if he tries to resurface again, how do I defeat him…my past, the old me, if he seems stronger than me?"

"It's okay, Asoya," Elisa says, as she walks over to where he is. She places her hand on his shoulder to comfort him. "I shall be asking the Lord to give you wisdom. I can't give you the answer to that question, why don't you ask the Lord and search His word for the answer?" Elisa says excitedly.

"Hummm…search His word," Asoya says, as he looks down upon the ground. "Ah, why does being a Word Carrier have to be so complicated?" he asks, with agitation in his voice.

"Is this the great, mighty and legendary Asoya that everyone once feared and spoke so highly of…is he now talking defeat?"

Asoya looks up.

"You are Asoya, Asoya the Candle. Remember, the Lord chose you, you didn't choose Him." Elisa pauses, then says, "Seek…Him."

Solitude

Back at his place of solitude, Asoya strikes his training bag. His attacks are as though he is raiding an area highly infested with ninja. His hits are cruel, delivering blow after blow, each strike harder than the last one he threw. A few of the rocks burst inside the tightly woven bag, from the weight of Asoya's fists, but he continues to train. He spin kicks the bag as he thinks of Ruthless Vermillion. The bag tears, splitting in two.

His foot remains in the air as all of the sand and remaining rocks that have not been crushed by his fist seeps to the floor. As the last bit of sand filters out, he lowers his leg gradually. He looks over at the candle that is on the other side of the room. The candlelight moves as though it is trying to escape the candle. Asoya's heart flashes red…'תקידב בל'…but this time it is so gentle that it is calming to him. A heart check. He examines himself.

"I am a candle," he says as he falls to his knees. He controls his breathing, slowing it down, and unrolls a scroll. He focuses on what is written in book of Philippians.

Philippians 2:13-15:

"For it is God which worketh in you both to will and to do of *his* good pleasure. Do all things without murmurings and disputings (*disagreeing, conflict*): That ye may be blameless and harmless, the sons of God, without rebuke, in the midst of a crooked and perverse nation, among whom ye shine as lights in the world."

"Lights," he says, looking up from the scroll. "Candles."

Asoya's Trip

It has been four months since Asoya was attacked by his past. He takes an eight-day trip to a town to bring God's word to it. After resting, Asoya carries God's word to those he feels directed to speak with, reading to them Philippians 2:13-15. That night, he goes back to the room he is renting, only to sense that someone is there, inside the room.

Upon sensing another presence, Asoya draws out his blade and asks as though he is issuing a command, "Who's there?"

There is quiet. Wherever Asoya's eyes move, his sword follows. He examines the room from the spot he is in, separating the outside noises from slight sounds that come from inside of the room itself. His stance remains unmoved, ready. He sees a shadow and the shadow moves, but very shrewdly as it softly pulls its sword from the sheath on its back,

"A ninja…" Asoya says quietly, as he takes out two stars and slings them both at the intruder.

The ninja swings his sword quickly, blocking them both. His reflexes are quick. This ninja is skilled. A hint of light touches the invader's sword, allowing Asoya to see what is written upon it. He recognizes the words on the blade.

"Vermillion," he says, realizing that it is his old nature/past-self standing on the other side of the room with his sword drawn, *dragon smoke*.

"You again," he says, annoyed, pointing the sharp end of his sword at his past. "What do you want from me? Answer now!" he shouts, demanding a response, but no response comes,

Asoya's past says nothing but stands there, staring at him with a devious smile, ready to strike.

"No matter," Asoya says as he positions himself in his fighting stance. "You will not have the victory…over me!" he says, frowning.

あなたは勝てないでしょう！

You will NOT have the victory over me!

決闘

Asoya's past dashes at him, swinging his sword. Asoya readies himself to deflect the blow. *CRASH!* The blow of his swing is so massive, it knocks Asoya's blade from his hand, nearly making him lose his balance. The sword spins, then sticks into the wall.

"What?" Asoya says, as he looks at his own hand with amazement.

He snaps out of it and quickly goes on the offense, ready to take down Vermillion using hand-to-hand combat. He punches his past in the face…but nothing happens. Asoya knees his past in the stomach…but his past just stands there.

"What's going on?" Asoya asks, as he backs up, kicking his opponent in the shoulder, but his past takes the hit as though Asoya is a small gnat. He then elbows his past self in the chest…but nothing happens!

My attacks have no effect on him, Asoya says to himself as he stands there, shocked to see that his attacks are to no avail.

"Ha, ha-ha ah ha, ha, ha, ha, ha…useless…" his past self says with delight.

With that said, Asoya's past knees him in the stomach, then spin kicks him in the face, causing him to spin upwards. As he is still spinning upwards, Asoya's past grabs him by his leg, then yanks him back down, catching him by the collar of his shirt, holding Asoya in the air. He dangles, squirming, trying to pry himself free from Ruthless Vermillion's grasp, but cannot. Ruthless Vermillion laughs, watching Asoya wrangle.

After a few moments of watching, he pulls Asoya slowly close to his face, then says, "You, I have overcome." His past looks at Asoya with a cold stare and empty gaze. He then throws him in the air, and kicks him in his stomach

Asoya bursts through the wall and slides on the grass outside. He rises up slowly with one eye swollen shut.

Struggling to stand, he says, "Ah, it's going to take…more than that to get rid of me!" he shouts with confidence, looking at his past without fear.

Asoya's past glares at him. His countenance goes from an eerie smile to a scowl.

"Nope…I will not be overcome…by you," Asoya says.

Asoya's past charges him and does a flying kick. Asoya closes his eyes, and with the little strength he has, he braces himself for the impact.

There is silence. Asoya opens his eye, only to see that his past has vanished. He looks around frantically.

"Where are you?" Asoya says to himself as he grits his teeth.

Seeing that his past is gone, he drops to one knee and says, "I can't keep doing this…" Then he passes out.

The Following Morning

The following morning, Asoya awakes to the sound of birds chirping and feels the cool breeze rush across his skin. He looks up and sees the sun's rays piercing through the leaves of the trees.

Asoya relaxes, takes a deep breath, exhales and says, "Today is a new day. Thank You, Master, for this day." Still lying on the ground, Asoya reaches up his hand to feel his face. "Huh? The swelling is gone? I must have been dreaming."

Getting up slowly, Asoya has a sharp pain in his stomach.

"Nope, it wasn't a dream," he says, as his eye twitches from the pain. "I miss the days when I was actually able to take out my enemies, but this, this is on a whole other level," he says, looking down at his hand. "Lord, I was wondering if there is a lesson You want me to learn from this?" He dusts himself off.

"Ah he…" Asoya chuckles. "I already know what Elisa would say, she would ask, 'Asoya, what have you learned from this experience?' Well Elisa, I would say I have learned not to fight with my past, and she will ask, 'Why not, Asoya?' And I would reply, because he will **win**! Ha, ha..."

Asoya then frowns and says, "I'm a Word Carrier, I should have had this conquered by now!"

He taps his right foot on the ground a few times after stretching, then slams it into the *hogyoku* tree that gives him shade from the sun's light. The tree cracks around his foot, then falls over.

"Why can I not harm my past if I can clearly plow through a tree?" he asks, looking at the large *hogyoku* tree on the ground.

So that the wood would not go to waste, he cuts it in several pieces and brings them to a carpenter so he can make bowls, cups and a few tables for him to give to the poor. He plants another tree where the other one was knocked over.

Asoya spends two more weeks in the town, then takes the eight-day journey back to the place where he was staying in hiding. Two days after his return, he goes by the orphanage to visit the children and see how Elisa is. The children are very excited to see him and ask him to tell them some short stories from the word of God.

Elisa is on the other side of the room, standing in the doorway, watching the other children who are playing outside. She turns and looks at Asoya. *Wow, he really is good with the children*, she thinks, and smiles.

After Asoya is done telling a few short stories, he does some training with Geto and those who desire to learn. He makes sure the children understand that what he is teaching them is for self-defense purposes only. They nod to let Asoya know they understand what he is trying to convey, as children often do when they are eager to learn something new.

When Asoya has finished his martial arts lesson, the children run excitedly outside to play with the other children who are already enjoying themselves. He sits down in a chair and begins to meditate deeply on the attack he had experienced on the journey he had taken prior to visiting the orphanage, thinking of a way to defeat his past.

Elisa, seeing that Asoya is disturbed, walks up to him and says, "Today is a wonderful day."

"Yes, it is," he says seriously.

"There are two children here who just amaze me and who I learn so much from. One girl's name is Laughter, and the other girl, her name is Smiles. They got those names from the other children."

Asoya sits quietly, listening to Elisa.

"Smiles smiles all of the time, and Laughter...well, she laughs all of the time," Elisa says with laughter in her voice. "Even though they are here in the orphanage, Laughter still finds time to laugh, and Smiles, ha, ha, she still smiles just as beautifully as she did when she was first brought here. I learn so much from those two..."

Elisa sighs, then continues, "I look at myself and ask, can I laugh today or can I smile even though I have had a hard and stressful day? It says in the book of Proverbs that 'A merry heart does good like a medicine.' What's in your heart, Asoya? What's in your heart that's causing your past to fight with you so?"

Asoya turns and looks at Elisa with amazement, because he feels as though she can literally see what is in his heart.

"What's in there? What is in your heart? 'A merry heart does good like a medicine.' A merry…heart," she says to him, with peace.

"A merry…heart…" Asoya looks down and places his hand over his heart as though he can feel what is in it.

"Well, I have to go check on the children. You know how little ones can be…we're going to have dinner in a couple of hours, you're welcome to stay if you'd like."

"Ah…I have word that I need to deliver."

"That's okay, some other time then. You know that you are always welcome here."

Asoya and Elisa both walk out the front door.

"Have a wonderful day, Asoya."

"You too Elisa." Asoya then throws his sword over his shoulder and walks off to the next town.

See you later, Word Carrier Asoya, she says within herself, then she turns around and tends to the children with the other workers.

笑い
Laughter

A merry (*happy*) heart makes a cheerful countenance (*face, expression or look*)...
(Proverbs 15:13)

A merry (*cheerful and happy*) heart does good like a medicine...
(Proverbs 17:22)

笑顔
Smiles

ハッピー
心臓
最高です
医学

The Medicine Man and The Light

Asoya walks on a trail that leads through the woods. While he is walking, he sees a man carrying a large wooden pack on his back...a medicine man 薬人.

"Greetings, traveler," the medicine man says as he turns and looks back at Asoya, for he hears Asoya's wooden *gata* sandals scratching across the dirt trail as he walks. "How is your journey going?" He turns his head back around and continues to walk.

"It has been very well," Asoya replies. He sees the man struggling to carry his heavy medicine pack, for the man has been walking for hours.

"I have plenty of natural remedies. Have you come for some?" he asks, excited that he might have another customer.

"No, I'm just taking this shortcut to get to another town."

"I need to rest," the medicine man says with exhaustion. "I've been walking and selling medicine for hours. I need to though, I need to sell a lot more, my wife is expecting a child soon." He stops to rest a little and sets his wooden pack on the ground. Asoya stops as well. "What town are you headed to, stranger?" the man asks, seeing if they are headed in the same direction.

"To a community not too far from here. There are people who need to hear the good news about the Savior."

"Savior?" the man asks as he counts his medicine inside of the wooden pack, making sure he hasn't lost any.

"His name is Jesus, and He is the Savior of all. He came to bring those who are in darkness out of it so that they can be in the light."

"Light?" the medicine man asks, captivated, never having heard such a thing before.

"Yes, light shines its brightest when it's in the shadows." Asoya then starts to laugh.

"What's so funny?" He cleans one of the medicine bottles on his shirt, then looks over at Asoya.

Asoya looks at the man and replies, "You and I are alone in the woods and you are carrying all of those goods. They can easily be taken from you. I have a sword, you have seen it, yet you are not startled in the slightest, nor have you flinched when seeing my countenance."

"Well, I'm in the people business," the man says with a smile. "Besides that, you don't seem very threating to me."

"You are right," Asoya replies. "But is not your business connected to the shadows?"

The man finishes putting all of the medication back into his wooden pack. "The shadows? I thought medications were a form of health and helped others," he says with his hand still inside his wooden pack, reaching for something...

"Take your hand out of that wooden pack now...ninja," Asoya says with seriousness as he looks at the medicine man, who is still kneeling down, reaching into his wooden pack.

"Ninja? You must be quite sleepy from your travels to speak such a thing. You are mistaken, sir." The man chuckles at Asoya's words.

He then quickly throws a star at Asoya, but Asoya is no longer there. The medicine man is not at all a seller of medications or herbs, but an assassin, an undercover ninja 潜入暗殺者. This undercover ninja is not associated with Asoya's old clan, but is from a rival clan.

"What? Where is he?" he asks as he reaches into his wooden bag and takes out more throwing stars. He also grabs a knife.

"Do you see these flowers?"

"Huh?" The ninja turns and sees Asoya pointing at a bed of flowers a few steps off the dirt trail.

"They bloom and grow best in the summer seasons, where there is much sunlight...the light," Asoya says, remembering how the Lord had brought him to the light.

The undercover ninja looks at the flowers, then back at Asoya.

"Just like summer is a season where things grow, it too is your time for growth. When you wake up, there will be a few scrolls lying across you. Read them and accept them."

The ninja pitches the star in his hand at Asoya, who quickly grabs a flare and throws it at the oncoming star. The two objects collide. There is a bright flash of light. The ninja covers his eyes, almost blinded. When the light goes away, he searches for Asoya.

Asoya taps him on the shoulder from behind him. When the undercover ninja turns around, Asoya disarms him, then strikes him three times on three parts of his body.

Once under the armpit of his left arm, then once on the wrist on his right arm, and lastly on the ninja's lower sternum. Asoya walks off. The ninja stands still, trying to gather what has just happened to him. He looks at his hands where the throwing stars used to be, then down at his sternum. Asoya walks in a circle in the distance, waiting for the ninja to fall…and fall the ninja does, to the ground, unconscious. Asoya stops walking in a circle, then returns to the ninja and looks down at him, frowning.

"I told you to take your hand out of that wooden pack," he says, and reaches down and grabs the man's shirt and drags him off the dirt trail,

"I am 'A Candle,'" Asoya says, as he props him up under a tree and places a few scrolls on the ninja's lap. He then continues his journey.

The Apple and Sugegasa

I n the following town, Asoya goes to the market area, purchases an apple, then leans against a tree located in the opening of the town and ponders on the words Elisa spoke concerning having a merry heart.

Asoya speaks to the Lord, saying, "Master, I feel as though there are many people in this town whom You want me to speak to. Who are they? Well…until You show me, I'm going to wait patiently right here and eat this apple." He then covers his head with a straw hat known as a *sugegasa* to hide his face, then begins to eat.

"Asoya!" a child cries from in front of him.

"Huh?" He looks down.

"I just knew it was you…Ha ha, you can't hide from me."

Recognizing Geto, Asoya says, "Little boy, what are you doing here? Where's Elisa?"

"Ah, she's somewhere. Hey, are we going to go on a mission today?"

"No, no mission. Go back to where you came from."

"When I get big, I want to be a Word Carrier too…just like you."

His words startle Asoya, catching him off guard. Someone actually wants to be like him in a positive way.

"Can I be like you, Asoya?"

Asoya does not respond, but stares at Geto. He is speechless and moved because someone actually wants to follow in his footsteps. Asoya then looks at his apple, sighs, relaxes his face, tilts his *sugegasa* up and looks back down at Geto, who is smiling from ear to ear.

He unsheathes his blade, cuts the apple in two, then says, "Here you go." He reaches his arm out, extending half of the apple to Geto.

"Really? Ha ha, wow! I love apples, they're my favorite," he says happily as he takes a big bite.

"Now, let's go find Elisa."

"Okay," Geto says as he takes another bite out of the apple.

Geto and Asoya walk around for hours, searching for Elisa.

Asoya finally asks Geto, "Where's Elisa?"

"Ummm, she's back at the orphanage."

"What?" he says in shock and amazement. "Why didn't you tell me this before?"

"Because I wanted to hang out with you."

"Huh?" Asoya says as he looks at Geto. Seeing the expression of joy on the boy's face and the twinkle in his eyes, Asoya takes off his hat, dusts it off and places it on the child's head.

As Asoya and Geto take the trip back to the orphanage, he makes the boy promise not to run off from the orphanage. Geto is curious as to why Asoya no longer wants him to run off. After Asoya explains the dangers that he could run into, Geto agrees quickly.

Asoya adds, "Besides that, you make Elisa and the other women who work there worry. I know God takes care of you, but do you want them to worry? Do you want Elisa to worry?"

"No," Geto says, with sadness in his voice.

"They care about you very much, that's why I'm telling you this. When I was your age, I didn't have anyone who cared about me the way these women do. You should be happy." Asoya winks at him.

Geto smiles as he tries to keep Asoya's hat balanced on his head. As they near the orphanage, Asoya hides behind a tree and signals for Geto to go inside. The boy smiles real big, hugs Asoya's leg, then runs to the house. As he runs, he notices he still has Asoya's hat, so he turns around, runs back to Asoya, hands him his hat and bows himself before him in reverence, as a student often does to his teacher.

"Thank you, *masutā* Asoya."

Masutā means master in Japanese. With that said, Geto turns around, and runs to the house. Asoya waits a couple of seconds behind the tree, puts his hat back on, ties it, then starts to walk back to his place of abode. Elisa is waiting inside patiently for Geto to return home. She has peace within herself because she prayed for him. Geto opens the door slowly, trying not to be seen.

As he gently closes the door, Elisa meets him and says, "Geto, where were you?"

"On a mission!" he says excitedly.

"A…mission?"

"Yep," Geto says happily. "But you don't have to worry about me running off anymore, I'm staying right here, with you." He runs up to Elisa and gives her a big hug.

"Huh?" she says, puzzled.

Geto then releases her and runs into the other room happily, and starts to play with the other children. Elisa smiles, and then walks into the room where the children are playing.

ワードキャリア

The Word Carrier

真実
持参人

For all have sinned, and come short of the glory of God; Being justified freely by his grace through the redemption that is in Christ Jesus: Romans 3:23-24

Heart Check

It is now evening and Asoya begins to do some training while reflecting on the events that happened throughout his day.

"Man," Asoya says as he does his sit-ups. "I had no idea that I had that much effect on the children, all they want to hear is stories." Asoya laughs. "And the little boy…all he wants to do is follow me. Jesus, You are my Master and Lord. You really are changing my whole outlook on things. I used to trust no one, but I'm now starting to trust Elisa, for she reminds me of the Word Carrier who was before me. He was just like Elisa, so welcoming, wise, humble and relaxed. I don't think I'll ever understand people like that."

Asoya continues. "You're even changing my heart regarding people. Not everyone is an enemy, as I once believed and was taught." He sits up to rest. "My sword…" He focuses on its location. "I cannot live by the blade and serve God too. This conflict within myself is maddening."

His chest flashes red.

"Ahhh…" Asoya says as he looks down and clutches his chest, as though he were holding his heart in the palms of his hands.

BOOM… Asoya's heart beats loudly. *BOOM…* With each heartbeat, his chest flashes and lights up light red. *BOOM…* Words appear in Hebrew across his chest, 'תקידב בל' which being interpreted translates to the words, *Heart Check* or *Heart Examination*.

Recognizing what it is, Asoya says, "Heart Check, it has been a long time since I've had one of those."

BOOM…

"So this is what was in my heart, Lord? Living by…the blade?"

BOOM…'תקידב בל'

"I guess…so…" Asoya says as his heartbeat returns to normal and the flash goes away. The Hebrew words turns invisible. Still holding his chest, Asoya thinks on his past attacks and his response to them both. Upon taking a deep breath and releasing the air, he commences to do some push-ups.

"Lord," he says as he does his pushups. "I realize now what was really in my heart. Secretly I had a desire to go back to my *old ways*, and because of that, I was reminded of my past self, who I no longer am. Anger, rage, and heartlessness…I don't want to go back to being any of those things. Forgive me, Master…I don't want that in my heart any longer. Elisa was right, You chose me, I did not choose You."

Asoya stops doing pushups, sits down, puts his hands behind his head and says, "Lord, I need help, how do I conquer my past when he seems stronger than I am? Please show me what I need to do."

He speaks with a frown on his face. With that said, wind blows Asoya's window open.

"Huh?" He raises his arm over his head and face to block the force of the wind, for the wind blows strongly and it is hard for him to keep his eyes open. "Ahh, what's going on?"

The wind blows Asoya's papers around, then it rolls open one of his scrolls with God's word written upon it. The scroll lights up, and out of it shoots a beam of light, from the scroll to the ceiling, then past the ceiling and through the clouds.

"Oh...No..." Asoya says, as he begins to panic.

The room is then consumed in light. He turns his head away from its brightness. When the light clears and the wind ceases, there stands an angel in front of Asoya where the scroll is located. Asoya turns back around, only to see the large being.

In fear he says, "Huh? Ahh...The Guardian...is here..." Asoya trembles.

"Hello, Asoya, I bring you word from the Lord," the angel says as he looks at Asoya.

"The...Lord?"

"Yes, the Maker of heaven and the heavens of heavens," the angel says with a smile. "And the maker of the earth and all that lives there in, all flesh must come to Him."

Seeing Asoya is fearful at his presence, the angel stretches his hand forward and says, "Do not be afraid. You have been speaking the words that the Lord spoke through the prophet Isaiah, saying 'Remember ye not the former things, neither consider the things of old. Behold, I will do a new thing...' but this is where you stop speaking, leaving out the other part of this verse which says, 'Behold, I will do a new thing; now it shall spring forth; shall ye not know it? I will even make a way in the wilderness, *and* rivers in the desert.'"

After a few moments the angel continues. "The things you are going through and have been experiencing are a form of wilderness, and the things pertaining to your past are a form of desert. Even in this, the Lord will make a way. I am here to show you one of those ways. You have been having a battle with your past...and it is due to two reasons, one of which you know. The first is from *your memory*. You remember how you used to be...who you no longer are. And the second is due to *the Sifter*..."

"The Sifter...who is this that you speak of?" Asoya asks.

The angel replies, "You know him as the dragon, but we know him as Satan, the Accuser of the brethren or the Sifter...the sifter of God's people."

There is quiet, but briefly. The angel resumes. "When Jesus walked the earth, Satan desired Peter, one of Jesus' disciples, to *sift* him like wheat, but Jesus the King of all kings prayed for Peter that his faith would fail him not. The same thing happened to Job, one of God's servants. The enemy tried to *sift* God out of him...but could not. He even tried to get Job to curse God, but Job would not."

"So...the enemy is trying to use my past against me, to try to sift me? Hummm, I see," Asoya says, with his hand on his chin, trying to take in what is being said.

"Ah, Guardian..." he says with hesitation. "Tell me, what do I need to do?"

"You fight." the Guardian says calmly.

"Fight...but how? I'm used to fighting with my hands, but this... this is different. It's...a..."

"Spiritual warfare," the angel says with a smile, because he sees Asoya is beginning to understand. "Ha ha, it is all right," the angel says with joy in his voice. "This is what I was sent here to tell you... you fight your past *with the word of God.*"

"With the word of God," Asoya says with a serious look on his face.

The angel is ready to depart from his presence, but Asoya forbids him by saying, "Wait..."

"Yes, Asoya."

"How do I fight my past...with the word of God?"

"The Lord told me you would ask me that, and He gave me the answer for you."

Asoya waits for the answer with expectation.

"It is written...that the word of God is quick, and powerful, and *sharper than any* two-edged sword."

"What?" Asoya says in amazement.

"It is able to divide asunder the spirit, soul, and body."

"It divides those things?" Asoya says with his hands on his forehead. "You must let me wield this blade!"

The angel laughs. "Redeemed One, the blade you are speaking of is *the Word of God.*"

And with that, the angel (*Guardian*) vanishes before his sight. Asoya pauses, then slowly makes his way to where the scroll is, which the Guardian had stood upon, picks it up and says, "The word…"

Still being a little shaken by his encounter with the Guardian, Asoya drops to his knees with one hand on the ground and the other still grasping the scroll.

"This word is Powerful, such power comes from it. I didn't realize how powerful this word was, and I have been carrying this…something that's *sharper* than a two-edged sword. How astonishing." Asoya pulls the scroll close to his heart, then bows himself upon the ground to give reverence to the Lord. While Asoya is kneeling before the Lord, the scroll lights up. Noticing the light, Asoya drops it. As the scroll shines forth light, golden words emerge from it.

"What's this?" Asoya asks, as the words begin to rotate in the air.

As they rotate slowly, Asoya reads them. "The word of God is… quick and powerful…sharper than any two-edged sword…these are the very words the Guardian just spoke to me."

BOOM...

Asoya's heart begins to beat loudly. *BOOM...*

His chest starts to flash light red. *BOOM...*

"Yes, Master...I understand now," he says as he closes his eyes and sits up, still being upon his knees.

BOOM...

"You don't want me to fight my past using natural means...but *with Your very word*."

With that said a beam shoots from Asoya's heart and goes to the ceiling, from the ceiling the beam shoots past the clouds. As this happens Asoya's hair begins to slowly rise and he begins to smile.

BOOM...

His heart beats again and the words rotating in the air start to slowly surround and circle him, like unto a barrier. Asoya inhales then exhales deeply.

"Lord, I receive Your words that were just spoken to me by the Guardian."

The words circling Asoya go around the room, then come back around to enter into his heart. Each time a word enters his heart, golden sparks flew from his chest. As the last word enters into his heart, he opens his eyes. The irises of his eyes glow like gold, then return to their normal color. His hair also goes back down to its normal state. Already on his knees, Asoya falls to his face and begins to breathe heavily. As he breathes, drops of sweat fall to the floor.

"Wow, this is true power! To have God's word *dwelling within you*," he says as he slowly stands up. "I'm not just carrying His word," Asoya looks at his hands, then places his hand over his heart, "but His very word is abiding in me…Ha ha, I am a Word Carrier."

He clenches his fist tightly. He then looks forward.

"When I see my past again," he chuckles, "it's over." Then his heart beats loudly and his chest flashes red one more time.

BOOM…

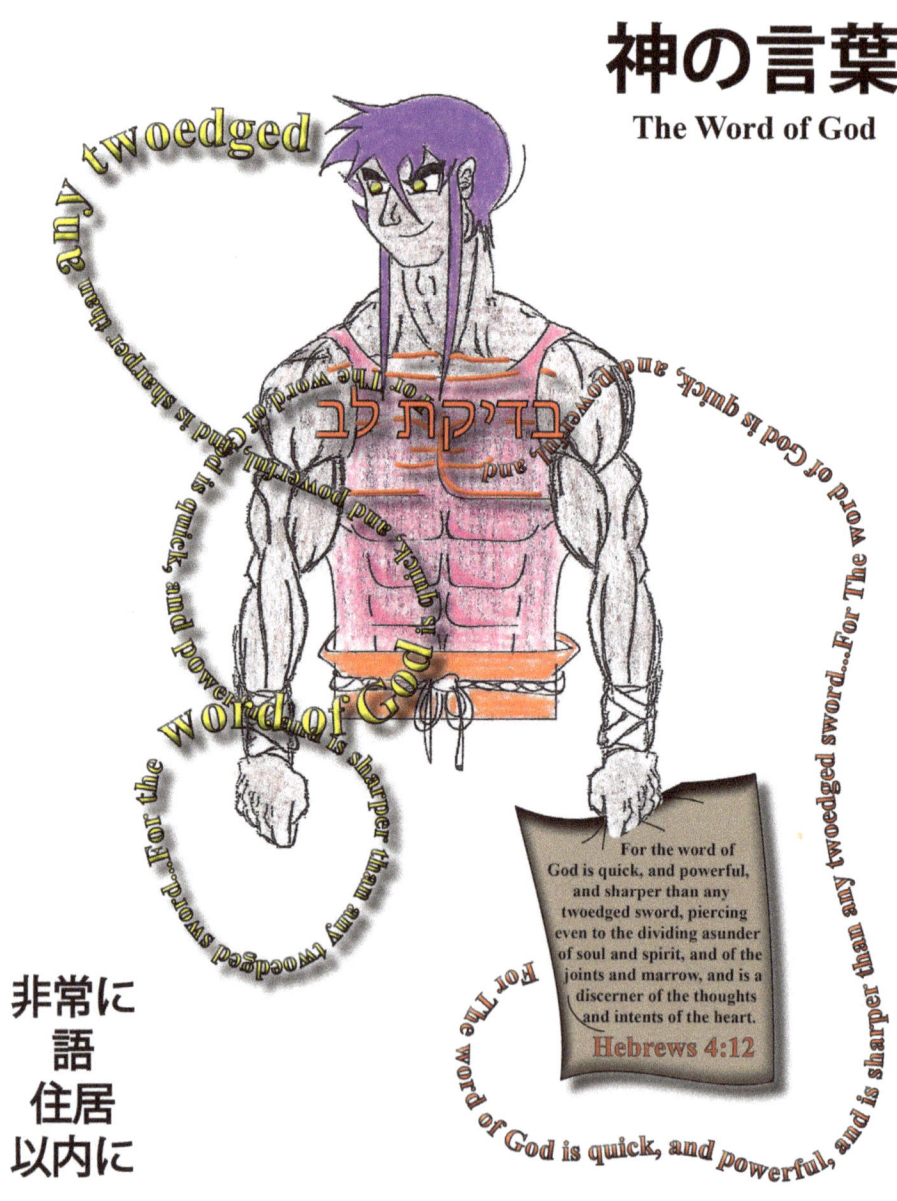

神の言葉

The Word of God

非常に
語
住居
以内に

For the word of
God is quick, and powerful,
and sharper than any
twoedged sword, piercing
even to the dividing asunder
of soul and spirit, and of the
joints and marrow, and is a
discerner of the thoughts
and intents of the heart.
Hebrews 4:12

Asoya and the Fisherman

Asoya pays a fisherman to take him to the other side of the river in his boat. As the fisherman rows, Asoya speaks to him about the word. The man tilts up his straw *sugegasa* hat as he listens to the words Asoya speaks. The man continues to row downstream as he listens. Asoya speaks to him about what the Lord said concerning the Kingdom of Heaven,

"Again, the kingdom of heaven is like unto a net, that was cast into the sea, and gathered of every kind: Which, when it was full, they drew to shore, and sat down, and gathered the good into vessels, but cast the bad away." (Matt. 13:47-48)

"The sea can represent the earth, and the fish different types of people from every nation on earth. The net is the gatherers of the fish and the Fisherman can represent the Lord, for He is a fisherman of all fisherman, and the fish which He catches are men themselves. When He casts His net into the sea, will you be ready to stand before Him?"

The fisherman says nothing, but ponders on Asoya's words as he rows.

"The question isn't will the net be cast into the sea…but will you be ready when it is."

There is a long silence.

"This is why we ready ourselves."

The fisherman stops rowing as he listens to Asoya. The boat continues to drift as the clear water moves gracefully back and forth.

"We must be…ready for what?" the fisherman asks.

"To stand before the one who made us all," Asoya says calmly.

The fisherman tilts up his hat, then gazes at Asoya before casting his gaze on the sparkling water.

"My job is to tell you about Him so that when He does gather His net, you will be ready." Asoya gives an illustration to the fisherman that he can understand. "The fish were swimming in muddy water. The muddy water can represent sin. Now this muddy water was killing them slowly, but they knew it not because they were used to swimming in it. They were so used to swimming in the muddy water that they thought that was their way of life. But the Fisherman knew this was not so. He designed them to swim in clean water with salt...not muddy.

"Clean water can represent life 人生, and the muddy water represents sin 罪. The muddy water was separating them from the Fisherman. This was a problem, so to solve this problem, He devised a solution: to send His Son into the world."

The fisherman sees another line being pulled, so he gets up and grabs the bamboo stick, pulling in the line. There is a medium-sized fish attached to the end of it. He stares at the fish, thinking of the words Asoya has just spoken.

Asoya continues. "The Fisherman saw that the fish He made were all headed in the wrong direction, so He sent His Son into the world to show us which way we are to go and to lead us in the right direction; to lead us from the muddy water to the clean water. Jesus is God's Son who was sent into the world. He became one of the fish—"

"God's Son became an actual fish?" he asks, misunderstanding Asoya's illustration.

"Not an actual fish," Asoya says, laughing. "Remember in this illustration, the fish represent a man. The Lord became a man. He is also known as the Word, and the Word became flesh, and dwelt among us. He became one of us." He reads from the scroll where it was written about the Lord becoming flesh. (John 1:1-14) "Do you understand?" he asks.

The fisherman nods, letting him know he understands his words. Asoya continues the illustration.

"Back to the illustration. He taught us how to be better fish and do those things that are pleasing in the eyes of the Fisherman (which represents God the Father). He taught us about the clean water and the muddy water, and tells us the difference between the two. He tells us to choose the clean…to choose life…eternal life. Then the fish who was sent into the sea, which was God's Son, died."

"He died? But...why would God's Son die?"

"Because of sin, our sins...because of the muddy water. He died and took on our sin, the muddy water so that we can live and swim in clean. He who knew no sin (which is Jesus) became sin. He died in our place so that we will not have to die. He sacrificed His life so that we can live and have newness of life, eternal life. But death could not hold Him. He resurrected from the grave after three days."

The fisherman catches another fish on his bamboo pole.

"I too was in the muddy waters of sin...but the Fisherman of all fishermen sent someone to fish me out. He made me new and clean, now I serve the Fisherman of all fishermen, the Creator of heaven and earth. Because I serve Him, my job is to fish others out of the muddy waters of sin."

"Those words are not for someone like me...I don't deserve to be clean. Maybe someone who has more money than me," the fisherman says, feeling unclean and unworthy to hear such words spoken.

"Money? This word that I carry is for everyone, the rich and the poor, the widow and the orphans, for all. For anyone who will receive it."

"Anyone?" the fisherman asks, as the heaviness and unworthiness he is feeling start to lightly lift.

"Anyone," Asoya says with a smile. "Come to Him and be made clean." (Matthew 11:28-29) (John 15:3)

As soon as this is said, they arrive on the other side of the river. The fisherman receives the Lord in his heart. Asoya then prays for him. The man silently cries. When he finishes praying for the man, he prepares to get out of the boat. As he gets out, the fisherman hands him three of the fish that he caught.

"No," Asoya says. "I don't want to impose on your business."

"It would be my honor if you took these," he says as he bows, still extending the fish.

Asoya grabs hold of the string tied to the fish. The fisherman rises.

"Besides, I'm going to be out here all day."

Asoya nods in agreement, then turns and starts to walk toward the forest. The fisherman returns to his boat. He hears movement and goes to where the noise is coming from. It comes from behind where Asoya had sat in his boat. The fisherman finds a large number of fish. Amazed, he counts and finds there are over seventeen fish lying on the floor of the boat.

Asoya smiles as he hears the fisherman's enthusiasm, for as he was talking to him about the Lord, Asoya was catching fish with his bare hands, placing them behind his back and setting them on the floor of the boat. Asoya heads to a town not too far from where the fisherman has dropped him off.

He spends many days speaking to them about the Kingdom of God and the power of God's word. After a few days, he finds a secret place behind the woods near a waterfall to meditate on the word of God.

Bright and dark pinkish flowers known as *shibazakura* or pink moss are everywhere. Asoya takes his sword from around his back and props it under a large *katsura* tree. Its leaves are bright green and almost glow in the evening sky as they sway in the gentle breeze. He walks a few steps away from the tree, then sits down on the ground. The sound of the crashing waterfall behind him is relaxing and peaceful. He closes his eyes and starts to meditate on the Word of God.

Asoya's Past

"I was wondering when you'd show your face again. You finally decided to come," Asoya says with both eyes closed as he thinks on God's word.

Asoya's past self steps out of the shadows, glaring.

"I was just thinking on God's Word. You're disturbing my meditation time, you know that?" he says as he opens one eye, looking at his past self, then closes his eye to continue meditating.

"You must have been mediating on your past...your past deeds. Them...you can't escape," his past proclaims as he watches Asoya sitting on the ground with legs and arms crossed. Asoya remains silent, focusing on the word of God. But his past continues to talk. "You...are an assassin..."

"I may not be able to escape you, but God has given me the tools to overcome you," Asoya says as he opens both eyes. He gazes at the *shibazakura* flowers in the distance.

"Tools...like these..." his past self says as he raises his sheathed blade and stars in the air, as though he were surrendering.

Asoya moves his eyes and focuses them on his past self, Ruthless Vermillion. "No, better," he says with a grin.

"Then," his past says as he puts his stars away, then ties the strings wrapped around his blade around him, allowing his blade, *dragon smoke*, to hang from his back, "let's put these new weapons to the test." He gets into an attack position.

"This time will be different," Asoya replies as he slowly rises to his feet. "You cannot defeat me."

Asoya's past stares at him with gloom. They ready themselves for combat. Both stay in their attack position, neither flinching. In the background, the sound of crashing water from the waterfall fills the air. His past speeds in his direction, laughing eerily. Asoya does not move, only grins as his past rushes toward him. Asoya sees an opening, so he takes it, balling up his fists. Asoya's fist smashes into his past's chest 胸板.

"I told you I was meditating on God's word."

Vermillion slides backwards from the hit but stays on his feet. He finally stops sliding and looks down at his chest where Asoya struck him, and sees a hollow fist imprint.

"What? You thought I was joking?" Asoya says with laughter in his voice.

His past self touches the fist imprint, then looks up at Asoya and grins.

"And on His word shalt thou meditate day and night…heh heh," Asoya says, quoting Joshua 1:8. "This book of the law (*regulation,* rule, statute, covenant or commandment) shall not depart out of thy mouth; but thou shalt meditate *(contemplate, ponder, think on/about, consider and reflect)* therein day and night, that thou mayest observe to do according to all that is written therein: for then thou shalt make thy way prosperous, and then thou shalt have good success."

Asoya thrusts his fists at his past's shoulders, then on his inner thigh. His past falls to one knee, sighs, then gets back up. His past looks over at Asoya's blade, propped up under the *katsura* tree. He punches Asoya, who blocks his fist using his elbow. His past's fist shakes from rage, seeing that his attacks have no power over him. Asoya looks his past in his eyes, smiles then jests.

"Heh heh…yeah. Joshua 1:8."

Asoya's past attempts to chop him on his shoulder with the side of his hand. Asoya takes a few steps back. The chop lands in Asoya's hand. He closes his hand, bending his past's wrist. His past again goes down to one knee. In anger, his past self yanks his hand free from Asoya's grip, then runs up his chest, doing a back-flip off of it, expecting to knock Asoya over. He lands on his feet from the flip. Asoya remains standing. He then looks down at his chest and dusts it off and asks, "What was that supposed to be?"

His past backs up slowly, then disappears into a shadow.

Asoya says, "I dislike bananas. I'll tell you why, they leave a funny taste in your mouth and at times have this strange stringy stuff that comes off of the banana and the banana peel. Now grapes, grapes I can do, with a side order of fish as a dish."

When Asoya says this, his past pokes his face out of the shadows and says, "Your past shadows…they are talking."

Asoya listens.

"Do you hear them? They are saying 'The only truth you know… is your blade!' Remember? O how many you have slain who have fallen on the edge of your sword's thrust."

Asoya looks back at his blade that is propped up against the *katsura* tree.

"It's right there, go on, pick…it…up…"

Asoya frowns. He turns his head around, looking at his past. The warfare continues their conflict. They battle for some time. The more Asoya entertains his past, the stronger it gets and the more his past speaks.

"The tools you have are no match for the tools I have," his past says as he smiles.

Remember

Asoya's past takes out a few throwing stars and throws them at Asoya. Each star has a different memory, a different regret. One of the stars hits Asoya. He slowly pulls it out as it lights up. Asoya looks at the star. He sees images from his past. He quickly looks at his past self, backs up, then back down at the star.

"Remember…" his past says to Asoya as he looks down at the glowing star.

The star plays a memory from Asoya's past. In the memory, Asoya was sent on a mission to take out a target. He traveled to the destination as he was ordered. He saw the man he was after. Rather than entering the man's home, he threw a star into the home from a distance, to wound the man before going in to finish the job. Though Asoya's aim was accurate and calculated well, he did not foresee what would happen next. A little boy was in a part of the house that Asoya could not see. The boy ran to his father. The star continued to spin, but instead of the target, it hit the small boy.

"Noooo!" Asoya shouted in the memory, as he saw that the star meant for his desired target mistakenly hit the young boy. He ran into the house and laid hold of the young boy. He was crying as he held the boy close to his chest. He pulled out the star, then left with haste. Asoya returned to his clan and laid the stars he used on his mistaken target before his master.

"You have done well," his master proclaimed, as he saw the blood-stained throwing star set before Asoya.

"I have failed you, Master," Asoya said, as he got down on both knees and placed both fists on the floor.

"How so?" his master asked, trying to understand Asoya's statement of failure.

"There was a young boy…no more than five years of age who was hit by a stray star. Master, I…"

"Enough! Put away those meaningless feeling, these sentiments. You are ninja, a weapon! We destroy anyone or anything that gets in our way. Such is the way of those who dwell in the shadows."

Asoya's eyes opened wide with amazement, stunned by the words he just heard his master express.

"But Master—" he said as he raised his head slowly to look at his master. Upon seeing the rage on his master's face, Asoya placed one hand over his chest and bowed. "Yes Master."

He then rose and left his master's quarters. He headed down the long hallway that was right outside the door of his master's quarters. A ninja with long blue hair, most of it covering his face, leaned against the wall in the hallway with his eyes closed and his arms crossed. In his crossed arms he held his sheathed blade.

When Asoya passed him, the ninja opened his eyes, frowned, then said, "It's going to be all right Asoya."

Asoya took a few more steps before stopping. Then he looked down at the ground, frowning and gritting his teeth. He gripped his sheath blade tighter and tighter. The veins in his arm bulged. He then turned and looked at the ninja with an empty gaze.

"Huh?" the ninja said as he looked into Asoya's eyes. Something was different, something was off. The ninja saw that something had broken in Asoya…something snapped. This was not the Asoya the ninja once knew. This Asoya was different. Callous…

"Ha ha ah ha haaaa! Look what we did," his past shouts, laughing, as he sees what Asoya did in his past.

Tears well up in Asoya's eyes, as he backs up, trembling, as the memory fades.

"That was the mission that changed you…when darkness overtook you and you fell into the shadows."

"Stop talking!" Asoya yells as he takes out a dart and casts it at his past.

His past moves his head and catches the dart between two fingers. He runs and throws a punch at his past, who catches the punch in his hand, then strikes Asoya on the chest and side between his ribs and hip bone. Asoya hits the ground and slides across the summer *shibazakura* flowers, then finally comes to a complete stop.

"That was the day that the highest ranking assassin came into fruition. No one outranked you in your clan. No longer moved by your emotions, your feelings were numbed, only moved by the swing of your blade, and you lived only for the purpose of your next mission. That was the day that I sprang forth, vicious, unrelenting. You are me and I...am...you."

"No, you are not me...you are...not..." he says, getting up off the flower-covered ground. Holding his side, he runs toward his past.

His past takes out a throwing star and sends it spinning at Asoya. It hits him in his abdomen. He quickly tugs on the star, pulling it out. As soon as he does, the star sparks twice in his hand then starts to glow brighter and brighter. He looks down at it.

"No," he says, seeing another past regret start to form.

"Remember..." his past self uttered.

In the memory, Asoya ran and leaped over a wall. As he cleared the wall, he spun in the air, and took out his blade from its sheath. The words *dragon smoke* ドラゴンスモーク were etched deeply in the metal. He held it like a dagger as he landed on the ground feet first. He slid on the dirt for a few feet, and sliced through his target's chest. He stopped sliding, blade extended in front of him. The guards shot arrows at him. He deflected them. The sword *dragon smoke* sliced through the oncoming arrows with aggression, with a certain rage that would not stop until every single arrow was broken. As Asoya cut the last arrow in two, one of the target's guards ran at him. Asoya uppercut the guard with his free hand without even leaving his position, launching the guard into the air.

A second guard came. Asoya spun around, elbowing the guard in his sternum 胸骨. *Crack!* The guard's sternum fractured as he hit the ground, lifeless. The first guard, who was sent flying into the air, finally came down. As he fell toward Asoya, Asoya lifted his knee. The guard landed on his knee, and his back broke. Asoya allowed the guard's body to hit the earth before he spun around, lifting his leg into the air, then brought it down hard. Asoya's foot landed in the center of his chest, crushing his chest and ribs. Asoya then dug his sword into the guard's chest, puncturing his lung.

Asoya pulled his blade out of the fallen guard. He rose slowly as he stared at the guard's motionless body. Blood dripped from the tip of his blade, from the tip of *dragon smoke* onto the ground. More guards came. Asoya smiled, then threw down a smoke bomb. The guards fired arrows into the thick smoke. The smoke cleared and Asoya, the assassin, had vanished.

"No," Asoya says, trembling as his past memories and deeds replay before his very eyes.

"Yes!" his past self says as he runs up to Asoya and jumps, doing a flying kick.

Asoya is hit. He flies backward, hitting a tree. He then hits the ground, still trembling from his own past deeds.

"This is what you did. This is what I did, what we did together! We."

123

As he gets up, his past throws another memory star at him. In the memory, Asoya was kneeling before his master, receiving his next mission. He bowed before his master and said, "An enemy of my master is an enemy of mine."

He entered a building and took out thirty-two men. Asoya was ruthless in wielding his blade, each blow precise. He returned to his clan and entered his master's quarters.

"Your foes will oppose you no longer," he said as he knelt before his master.

Asoya stops looking at the memory of past deeds and turns to his past self. He takes out his dagger and punches upward with his free hand to hit his past self. He misses, then lifts up his knee to try to hit his past self in the side. He misses as he follows through with an upwards kick, then swings his dagger at his past. His past ducks as Asoya slices through one of his past images that his past cast at him. He punches downward. His fist smashes into the ground.

"Ahhhh!" he yells in anger, unable to strike his past, his accuser, his shadows.

Asoya's past is beating him up. He punches and kicks Asoya, and when Asoya retaliates, his past self takes out a star with another past memory and hurls it at him, rendering him powerless. Asoya crashes into the tree that his blade is under. He hits back first from his past's kick. He falls; his blade also falls right beside him. He gazes at it then gets up. Another star hits Asoya.

In this memory, a man walked outside at night and hearing a commotion from the bushes, thought it an animal. Once he went outside, he picked up a stick and walked past a shadow. He heard a voice speaking from the shadow.

The voice said, "Stop walking…turn around, but do not make a sound."

The man was petrified, for he heard tales of shadow whispers. If you heard a whisper coming from a shadow, a ninja was upon you. *A ninja!* the man thought, knowing he was in the presence of a mercenary. He dropped the stick he was holding.

"Who are you?" the man asked as he turned around slowly, non-threatening, as his voice went up in pitch due to fright.

The voice from the shadow spoke again. "Ruthless Vermillion." The voice speaking from the shadows was Asoya, revealing the name he was given in the clan. He stepped out of the shadows and unsheathed his sword called *dragon smoke*.

"Please…you don't have …to…do this," the man said, begging with fear, seeing a ninja with a drawn weapon. He saw the words written on his sword.

"The enemies of my master are the enemies of me…this is what my master ordered," he said as he raised his blade above his head. A massacre followed.

In the midst of the memory, Asoya's past self speaks. "This is what you did. What I did…we."

The Truth and the Shield

Asoya squeezes the grass, pulling some of it up with the dirt as he tries to pick himself up off of the ground and escape the memory.

"I am you…and you…are…me. Ruthless Vermillion." He smiles sinisterly. "We are Ninja…weapons."

Asoya turns his head toward his sword lying on the ground a few feet beside himself.

"You cannot escape me…we…equal perfection, assassin," he says, with his head tilted to the side, watching Asoya struggle with his past.

The sound of water flowing and crashing to the rocks below from the waterfall fills the air. Asoya starts to reach for his sword. The devil is standing in a shadow among the trees, looking at Asoya lying on the ground. The devil's eyes are red, glowing in the dark as he stares, like molten lava.

Asoya's past turns his head toward the woods and sees the devil standing in the shadow. Asoya's past lowers his head to the enemy to pay him respect, then raises his head again. The devil smiles. Asoya's past turns and looks back at Asoya, who is still on the ground. His past draws out his blade and slowly walks toward Asoya as he sees him struggling to reach for his own sword encased beside him.

悪魔
The Devil

ふるいにかける
The Sifter

Asoya tries his best to get up off the ground but cannot. He scratches across the ground, reaching for his encased blade. His fingers tremble and his hand shakes as he reaches for the one thing he once took comfort in…solace in: his blade. As he reaches for it, golden letters appear before his face. The letters begin to twirl around his eyes, causing then to light up gold.

Golden words begin to rotate slowly around the cornea and the iris part of his eyes…Asoya's heart beats and flashes red as his past brings down his blade upon Asoya. The earth shakes as if there is an invisible force field around Asoya, preventing his past from stabbing him.

"What?" his past says, trying to push the sword down to stab it through Asoya's back, but he can't. Something is keeping his sword back from touching him. His past sees words floating around Asoya's body and slowly twirling up his blade. They read, "If any man be in Christ…he…is…a New Creature!"

His past tries to shake the words off his blade, but cannot. He releases the blade, then looks back at Asoya. The words Asoya meditated on proceed from his heart and shield him. As it is written, "His truth shall be thy shield and buckler." (Psalm 91:4) *His truth shall be your shield*. The words then hit his past, knocking him back several feet from Asoya.

彼の真実はあなたの盾になります

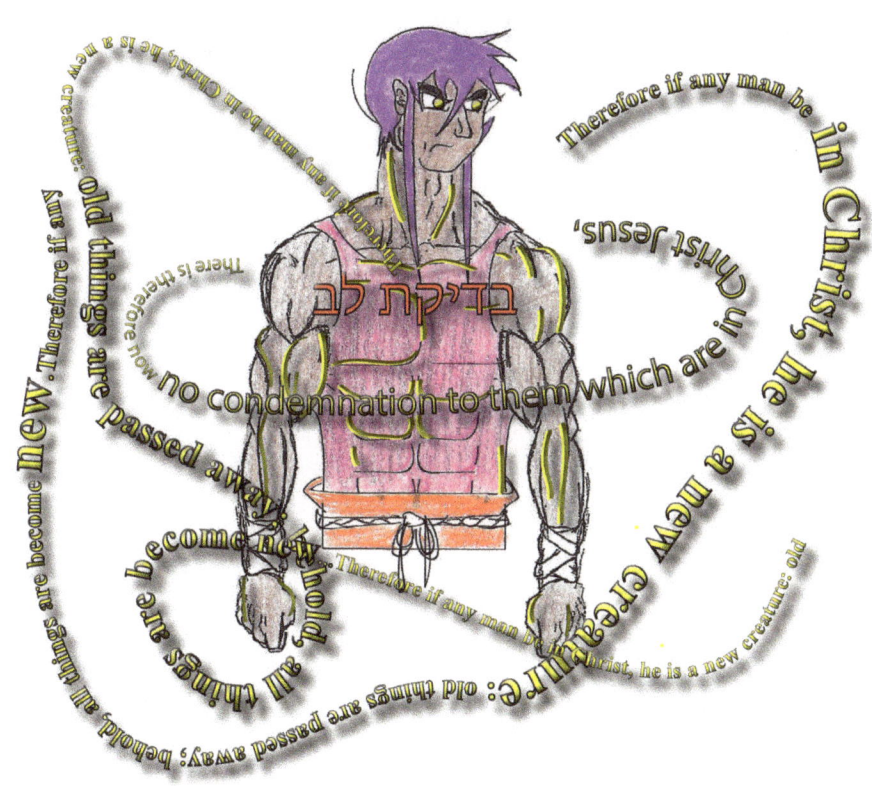

...his truth shall be your shield...
Psalm 91:4

Asoya slowly rises to his feet, laughing, realizing that God's word shield him. Golden words rotate around Asoya's body, forming a barrier that reads: "Therefore if any man *be* in Christ, *he is* a new creature: old things are passed away; behold, all things are become new." (2 Cor. 5:17)

"I am in Christ, and have been made a new creature by him," he says, walking slowly toward his past. His past takes out memory stars and casts them at Asoya, but those stars crash into the word that is shielding him, then fall to the ground. More words proceed from Asoya's heart and rotate around him.

They say: "*There is* therefore now no condemnation to them which are in Christ Jesus." (Rom. 8:1)

His past backs up upon seeing those words, then balls up his fists in anger. His past's eyes turn red.

"You are trying to condemn me, by showing me images and reminding me of things that I did in the past, but that Asoya...is no longer!" he shouts.

As he shouts these words, the ground shakes, knocking his past self off his feet.

"Old things have passed away, my past and who I used to be. And behold, all things are become new. I have been made a new person. I am a new man because I am in Christ."

"No you are **not**!" his past shouts, pushing himself up off the ground, and runs up to Asoya, attempting to punch him in his face.

His fist sparks as it crashes into God's word, which shields Asoya. His past looks confused as he sees that his fist can no longer touch Asoya.

"Hahaha, it's Kingdom stuff…it's Kingdom stuff," Asoya says, chuckling, seeing that God's word shields him yet again from his past's attack. He sees that things operate differently for those who are part of God's Kingdom, for those who are part of the Kingdom of God. His past picks up his sword off the ground and strikes Asoya several times, but the blade does not touch him. He is shielded.

"For the weapons of our warfare_are not carnal. We don't fight with natural weapons, the sword, the star, but the weapons that we do fight with are mighty…mighty through God to the pulling down of strongholds, things that have a strong hold upon us and our lives. And you, old friend, are a stronghold that's trying to take hold on my life, for you have a strong hold on me and you are about to be pulled down!" Asoya says as his eyes light up gold. God's word surrounds him like a shield. (Psalm 91:4) Asoya knocks the sword from his past's hand.

"You were trying to get me to trust in my blade as I once did, rather than trust in my new Master, who is the Lord."

His past backs up, then gets into an attack stance.

"This word that I carry, that is dwelling within me, is more powerful than you…my past."

Asoya moves his eyes upward, glancing at the sky, looking into the heavens. His eyes continue to glow like gold. The wind starts to push, but pushes mildly, moving across the pink flowers and grass. There is a calm. The leaves on the trees move like the ripples of water in the ocean. The only sound is the collapsing of water from the waterfall. A fish leaps out of the water, lunging for a fly passing by, and after a moment of being suspended in the air, it splashes back into the water.

Asoya takes his eyes off the heavens and looks at the word that surrounds him like a barrier. He then glances over at his past. His past takes out more memory stars to throw at Asoya, but after looking at the word dwelling within Asoya, and seeing the look in his eyes, his past drops the stars on the ground.

"See," Asoya says, as he sees that his past self can no longer harm him. "I found a new shadow to hide under, the shadow of the Lord, the shadow of the Almighty," (Psalm 91:1) he says with calmness.

His past is silent and cannot speak. His past starts to tremble.

"You are a shadow, a shadow of who I used to be…a shadow of my former self."

"I…am…you," his past says in a faint and broken tone, as if the wind has been knocked out of him.

"No, you are not," Asoya says gently, knowing he is not his past.

His past sees he cannot gain the victory over Asoya. His past drops to his knees and bows before Asoya, then rises and disappears.

Asoya Victorious!

Asoya looks up into the night sky and speaks to the God of Heaven:

"Lord, You and You alone have given me the victory. The victory to overcome my past…through Your word, with Your word."

He then falls to his knees and worships the Lord. The Serpent, also known as the devil or Sifter, backs up slowly, for he is enraged.

Enraged that he is unable to sift God out of Asoya using his device of trying to use his past against him. Black and gray smoke rises from his eyes as they fill with blackness. He disappears into the forest, seeking someone to devour…someone to sift.

The next day, Asoya goes back into the town where he has been sharing God's word.

"In God I will praise his word, in the Lord I will we praise his word!" (Ps. 56:10) he says as he gives thanks to the Lord before the people concerning God's word. He then continues to proclaim to them the power of God's word; the power that the Lord has given to overcome the past through His word. He tells them that sometimes when they are following the Lord, their past might try to rise up and fight against them, but he shares with them that the Lord has given them the tools to overcome their past, His word.

"Praise him for his mighty acts: praise him according to his excellent greatness," (Ps. 150:2) he says, telling the people that one of the mighty acts of the Lord is proving a way for those who trust in Him to gain the victory over their past. "In God I will praise His word, in the Lord we praise His word!"

The Golden Plated Throwing Star

Asoya rests, then gets up the following morning and fixes himself some breakfast. He cooks the last of his eggs and mixes them with his noodles. After eating his breakfast, he packs his bags for his two-month trip to the town where he feels led to travel. After packing, he leaves his hidden abode and starts on his travels. An hour into his journey, Asoya takes out a map to see what routes he needs to take. As he reads the map, a sharp object flies past his head and embeds itself into the tree he is walking past.

Still looking at the map, he says, "Humph, I don't have time for this. I don't know where you came from ninja, but if I were you, I'd run…now. Unless of course you came to hear the word," he says as he takes his sights off of the map and focuses his attention on the sharp object embedded in the tree beside him. It is a throwing star plated in gold. Recognizing the unique shape of the star and the markings on it, he says, "I'd recognize that star anywhere, Trang."

He turns and looks at Trang, who is standing inside a shadow, lying in wait.

"Do not speak my name as though there is a truce between us," Trang says as he lowers the mask covering his nose and mouth. He then pulls the hood back that is covering his head. Trang has a throwing star in his hand. It shimmers. He looks down at it, then back at Asoya. "There are no truces for the ones who scurry away and run from the clan, not even for Asoya the highest ranking amongst us."

He throws the star at Asoya in anger. Asoya's dagger smashes against the star, repelling it, causing the star to twirl back toward Trang. Trang catches it.

"I haven't seen you in over eight years. You were assigned deep undercover work in the northern quadrant of Japan while I was assigned solo missions in the southern," Asoya says as he lowers his dagger, then puts it way. "You trimmed your hair. This look suits you, and Trang, you know that you outrank me...everyone in the clan knows this. You just chose to allow Master to give that title to me rather than award it to you."

"That is because you were like my younger brother," Trang says with sadness as he looks at Asoya. Trang puts his throwing star away.

For an entire minute there is silence. Noticing Trang's sadness, Asoya says, "The clan taught me many things, but you, when it came to fighting with or without weapons, you were my teacher, and you were the reason I was feared in the clan due to the methods you taught me. Combatives 戦闘…I had deeply hoped they would not send you to fight against me, Trang."

"**Stop** speaking my name!" Trang shouts as his sadness turns to anger at Asoya's disloyalty to the clan. "Who said that they sent me? The time for formalities has long passed, and that day was the day you tried to burn the place that fashioned you into a weapon… to the ground."

"Past," Asoya says. He realizes that he won't be able to reason with Trang, for Trang's zeal and dedication to the ways of the shadows are strong, far stronger than Asoya's were when he was a member of the clan. "It's funny that you mentioned the past, because I just finished battling with my past self, and that indeed was a battle. I don't have time to get into a skirmish with you. I have kingdom work to do."

Trang pulls his sword from its sheath as though it were burning his back, then points it at Asoya. "Time. Oh, you better make time," he says as he gets into his attack stance. "Whatever friendship we had means nothing now. You betrayed the clan you swore to uphold!"

After hearing Trang's word, Asoya thinks briefly, then speaks. "Jesus said, 'swear not at all.'"

"Huh…Jesus? What is this that you are speaking?"

"Yeah, you're right, though," Asoya says as he stretches and yawns. "Whatever friendship we had in the natural has passed, for

I am in the light, and carry a weapon that is more powerful than any natural sword."

"What?" Trang asks as he looks down at this own sword, trying to understand Asoya's meaning.

"It's kingdom stuff, it's kingdom stuff, I'll…tell you about it later."

"You dare to— "

Asoya interrupts, "Assassins are taught numerous things, one of which is to lie in wait, allowing the shadows to conceal you… then strike your opponent down when they least expect you to. I am on my way to bring God's word to the people in another town and you are preventing me from doing so. The Sifter — have you heard about the Sifter? Because you're doing his work, you know."

"The Sifter, who…what is that?"

"It's kingdom stuff, it's kingdom stuff, I'll…tell you about that later."

"If you say that one more time," he says, taking out a golden plated throwing star and scrapes it across the sharp end of the sword that was in his hand, the sword sparks. Trang looks down at his star and after a moment points his sword at Asoya.

"You threw a star at me, not once but two times, and have drawn your sword to fight against me, and you're the one who's angry? It is good seeing you again, Trang, though my desire was not to see you in this manner."

"Those words shall be your last!" Trang shouts. He points his sword at the ground, then takes out four more throwing stars.

Seeing the stars, Asoya says, "Humph, I wouldn't do that if I were you. I just told you I recently had a battle with my past self, I'm not in the mood for tussling."

"Ahhh, that's it!" he shouts, throwing the five stars at Asoya.

Asoya dodges three stars while knocking the other two away from his body using his dagger. Trang then rushes Asoya with a vengeance, not as a former brother…but a nemesis 宿敵.

"I do not desire to fight with you, brother," Asoya says to himself as he reaches behind his back into his pouch and pulls out a smoke bomb. *BOOM*! Asoya crashes the bomb to the ground. It ignites with a few flickers and flashes of light. Thick smoke rises upward and outward, covering that area like a storm cloud that rushes in, blocking the light of the sun. When the smoke clears, Asoya is gone, and Trang is left wondering where he went. As Trang begins to look around, he notices some paper on the ground in the spot where Asoya was standing. He reaches down and picks it up.

The words written upon it say: *I apologize that I had to leave you, but I have business to attend to. I'm a Word Carrier now and must bring God's word to the people.*

At the end of those words there is a scripture: "Remember ye not the former things, neither consider the things of old. Behold, I will do a new thing…" (Is. 43:18-19)

Upon reading those words, Trang crumples the letter that is in his hand, looks up and says, "You have business, you say? We shall see if you've forgotten what the clan has taught you." Trang tosses the paper aside, looking over at a shadow cast from one of the trees. "Asoya...I will see you again, old friend."

Trang raises the cloth that is around his neck to cover his nose and mouth, then sheaths his sword, pulls the hood over his head, and jumps into a shadow.

元先生

Former/ *Past* Teacher

私たちの間に休戦はありません！

Word Carriers and Candles
蠟燭

Everything has a core, something that makes it what it is and function the way that it does. Cores apply even to those who are named amongst the Word Carriers. The core of those who are titled Word Carriers is to be a candle, a candle emitting light. They shine brightly amongst the darkness, leading others to the True Light, Jesus the Messiah, the Son of the Living God. Word Carriers are travelers. Whether the people are near or far, they travel to where the people are, bringing and making known the truths that God has spoken in His Word to the people who are around them.

They have autonomy, freedoms and life. This is because of what Jesus has done, giving His life for the sins of the world. Concerning Word Carriers, things try to assuage them, but as lights they prevail. As lights, Word Carriers overcome. They overcome despite their past and prevail despite past shadows. This is due to them choosing to fight — not fighting using natural weapons that have been forged by the hands of men, but by the very word of God.

As it is written:

"For the word of God *is* quick, and powerful, and sharper than any two-edged sword, piercing even to the dividing asunder (*apart*) of soul and spirit, and of the joints and marrow (*a person's body*), and *is* a discerner (*detector, scanner, analyzer, tester and examiner*) of the thoughts and intents (*ideas, plans and intentions*) of the heart." (Heb. 4:12)

The word of God is so powerful, it is able to tell/reveal what is in a person's heart, and separate the thoughts and hidden intentions within it. This is the very weapon and word that Word Carriers carry.

Asoya travels on. He smiles as he takes out a scroll, looking down at it. He then looks up, watching the trees slightly sway back and forth.

"The season of Netsu," he says as he looks up at the sky, seeing the clouds glide across the summer sky. He puts the scroll away and continues his journey to the next town, teaching others the power of God's word.

The end of *Asoya*: **Shadows from the Past**
(過去からの影): *Section 2*

天然武器

Natural Weapons

溶接
鋼

冷酷

The weapons that we *fight* and wage war with are not *natural weapons*...but are mighty through God. The weapons we fight with are able to pull down strong holds and *things that have a hold of us in our lives*. (2 Corinthians 10:4)

過去

TRANG

影

ハートチェック
Heart check/Heart Examination

בדיקת לב

(Hebrew)Heart check

Psalm 19:14

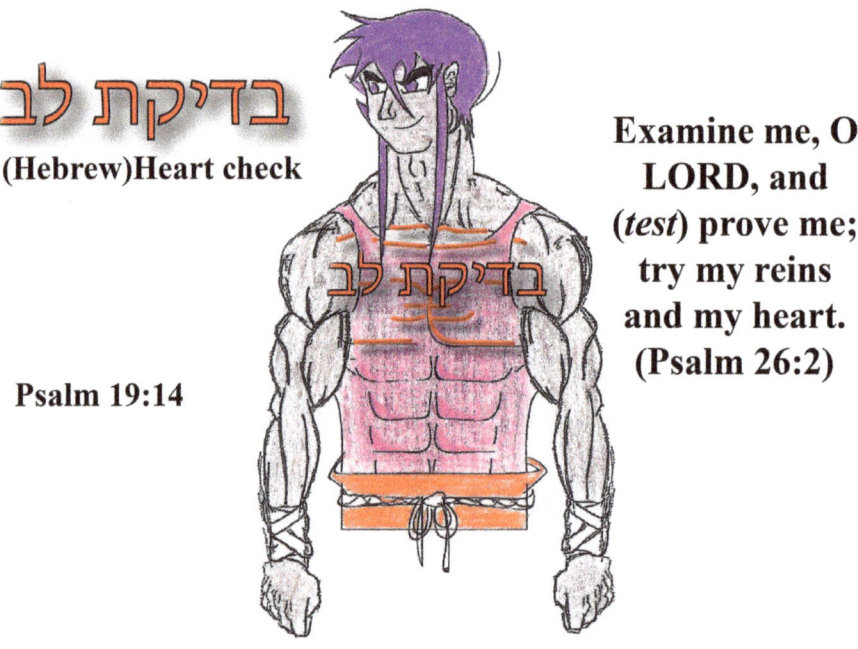

Examine me, O
LORD, and
(*test*) prove me;
try my reins
and my heart.
(Psalm 26:2)

(*Examine*) Search me, O God, and know
my heart: try (*test*) me, and know my
thoughts: And see if there be any
wicked way in me, and lead me in the way
everlasting.
(Psalm 139:23-24)

JESUS 治療者

Jesus

God the Son emptied himself of His glory and came down from heaven to earth and was born as one of us. Wrapping Himself in flesh, He is able to identify with us. He is the Messiah (キリスト). This was done because of sin; due to sin, God's creation has strayed and lost their way, so God the Father (父なる神) sent Jesus to lead us back to The Way that is right. He also became the atonement for our sins because we could not pay for them on our own. If we accept his sacrifice that He willingly made for us, we will have life-everlasting (永遠の命) and will come from darkness to the light.

Specializes in:

Healing those who are sick, mending the broken hearted, raising the dead, casting demons out /spirits that are evil, giving life eternal to those who believe on Him, preaching and teaching truth (真実), delivering those who are bound and leading those who are in darkness…to light. (This is just a brief list)

Weapons of choice:

- His Words ことば
- Became a sacrifice one time for all. 犠牲
- Love 愛

過去からの影

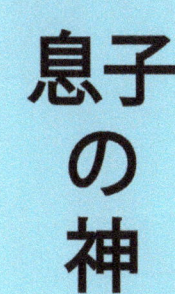

息子の神

More Stories Available Soon From Joseph DaVaulia

Asoya; From Darkness to Light
Asoya; Shadows From the Past Part2 Trang
Asoya; Uninitiated Affiliations
Asoya; Uninitiated Affiliations Part 2 The Ninja and the Samurai
Hatogi; The Japanese Ancient
Geto; Blessed Are the Peacemakers
Asoya; Hostilities Of The Adversary
B.F.O.B.F.; Goshen the Warrior
B.F.O.B.F.; Salvation Over Spinning Funnels
B.F.O.B.F.; The Fiery Darts of the Wicked One
B.F.O.B.F.; Sweet Tea yea!
B.F.O.B.F.; Love Your Enemies
P.V.; The Land Where Anything Goes
P.V.; Flaming Union
Parch'er Then a Desert

About the Writer/Illustrator

Joseph DaVaulia is a German American writer, artist, graphic designer and street minister. He is the founder of *Flares Amidst Shadows*. Flares are a form of torches, a signal used to give people light who are in danger, either having difficulty seeing due to the absence of light, or thick darkness. Flares are also used as guides. This is the purpose of *Flares Amidst Shadows*, to be that candle-light, that flare that *blazes brightly* to help others see. One of the avenues used is written stories, which are a teaching tool to help those who feel they are stuck in the dark and need help/guidance coming out of it.

Flares Amidst Shadows ™

Matthew 5:15-16

煌々

Praise God
Win Souls
Blaze Brightly

Isaiah 43:18-19

過去　　　　影

**Do not remember the former things,
neither consider the things of old.
Behold, I will do a new thing...**